STEVE MADDOX'S THOUGHTS ABOUT DANIELLE

It wasn't until I saw her again that I finally understood it wasn't stubbornness or pride that kept us apart. I left for the bright lights of the city, while she kept the home fires burning for me at the ranch. Well, I succeeded, all right—beyond my wildest dreams. But not all of my dreams came true: she never came to me....

DANIELLE HARTMAN'S THOUGHTS ABOUT STEVE

Why couldn't he see that I had no choice but to marry someone else, to go on with my life? The problems that separated us ten years ago were real...and now that he's back, they're still there between us. Only one thing is certain: I've never stopped loving him....

Please address questions and book requests to: Harlequin Reader Service
U.S.: 3010 Walden Ave., P.O. Box 1325, Buffalo, NY 14269
Canadian: P.O. Box 609, Fort Erie, Ont. L2A 5X3

Reunited Hearts

WESTERN *Lovers™*

GEORGIA BOCKOVEN
TRACINGS ON A WINDOW

Harlequin Books

TORONTO • NEW YORK • LONDON
AMSTERDAM • PARIS • SYDNEY • HAMBURG
STOCKHOLM • ATHENS • TOKYO • MILAN
MADRID • WARSAW • BUDAPEST • AUCKLAND

To Mary Ann Stephens. She taught me
what bravery was all about.

HARLEQUIN BOOKS
225 Duncan Mill Road, Don Mills,
Ontario, Canada M3B 3K9

ISBN 0-373-88532-6

TRACINGS ON A WINDOW

Copyright © 1984 by Georgia Bockoven

Printed in U.S.A.

1

AS GLARINGLY AS CHALK marks a clean blackboard, vehicle tracks marked the dry Nevada earth surrounding the old ranch house. Danielle Hartman's throat tightened convulsively. Unconsciously her hand went to the sun-bronzed triangle of flesh at her open collar as she stared at the scene below her.

Stretched out at the base of the hill where she stood was the remnant of a once-prosperous ranch, a ranch that was slowly being reclaimed by the patient, persistent desert. Sagebrush had crept ever closer until it replaced what at one time had been a carefully tended rose garden beside the old house, stealing in the process even the small amount of moisture needed to keep the poplar trees alive. On the house itself were large patches of bare wood where the white paint had peeled, creating stark wounds.

Each year as Danielle had watched the place she loved die its quiet unprotesting death, a part of her had died with it. Now, at what was sometimes an ancient-feeling twenty-nine, she occasionally felt as empty in spirit as the Maddox ranch was in actuality.

As if drawn by a macabre beckoning finger, her gaze wandered toward the road, where in the distance she saw wisps of dust lingering in the still air. Her mind again recoiled at the undeniable evidence that someone else had been at the ranch. Her hands curled into fists at her sides. *Dammit,* she vowed, *I will not let the last bit of him disappear. It's all I have left. If I let them take this, I'll have nothing.*

She blinked against the desert glare, letting her eyes stay closed longer than necessary in a weary mental sigh. Slowly she opened them again to look at the ranch. After ten years of being its unofficial caretaker she had almost come to think of the Maddox place as her own. It was here that she came on quiet mornings and lonely evenings to painfully remember what she had once tried so very hard to forget.

And now, if things went according to plan, the house she loved would soon become an easily leveled bump in the path of a dispassionate bulldozer—a bulldozer on its way to creating a new star in Nevada's gambling constellation.

Danielle removed her hat and wiped the back of her hand across her damp forehead. It was going to be a killer of a day, one that would bake the earth even drier than it had been the week before, every brown bush potential kindling, ready fuel for any stray bolt of lightning. She glanced at the Sierra Nevadas to the west, the distant peaks still mantled in the remnants of a record winter snowfall. The sky was clear of the often dangerous thunderclouds. Now if no one decided to use the side of the road as an ashtray the countryside might make it through yet another day.

Before putting the weathered Stetson she had inherited from her father back on her head she slapped it against her thigh. A miniature cloud of dust resulted, and she tried to remember the cool shower she had taken earlier. She had planned to arrive at the meeting as clean and "ladylike" as possible, but before she'd even had breakfast, a downed section of fence and an obstinate Hereford had left her looking as if she'd already spent a day chasing strays through the Pine Nut Mountains.

A soft sigh whispered through her full, slightly parted lips. She knew that by the time she finally arrived at the meeting in Weberstown, sweat and dust would combine to make her look as though she hadn't bathed in days.

That damn meeting. Just knowing it was coming had been like having a gremlin sitting on her shoulder gleefully reminding her of dreams that had died. Every time she thought about the reason for the meeting her stomach tightened in suppressed anger. *As if Nevada needed another place for the world's wealthy to play with their money.*

And what would happen to her own ranch when this new miniature city was created? With more than a third of her borders shared by the Maddox place she didn't hold out much hope that she would be able to keep things even remotely the way they were now. How long would she be able to live with that kind of circus next door, remembering that at one time the entire valley had held only the population needed to run two ranches?

Damn you, Steve Maddox. How could you sell your land to an outfit like Eagle Enterprises? How could you let something like this happen?

She eased her hat back on her head, tucking long wisps of sun-bleached brown hair under the sweat-stained crown with the tips of her fingers. "And how," she unconsciously, painfully whispered aloud, "could you stay away for ten years?"

Danielle took one last look before she climbed back into her beryl-green pickup with the double H on the side. Without purposely thinking of her actions she reached forward to start the engine and turn the wheel, until the truck was once again headed for the neighboring valley and Weberstown.

On the way into town she tried to shake the feeling that attending the meeting at the Pioneer Valley Church to further "discuss" the developer's plans for Maddox ranch was an exercise in futility. She had to give the effort one last shot, she told herself. At least this time she was going with some solid ammunition—something a little more convincing than an impassioned speech about the destruction of the "rural" atmosphere of the region should the casino be built. Perhaps, when the townspeople and outlying ranchers heard how much of the area's precious water supply would go into the project, she would win a few more converts to her side.

STEVE MADDOX STOOD in the shade of a giant poplar tree at the edge of Weberstown. Although he had purposely dressed in faded jeans, plaid western shirt and old boots in order to blend in with the townspeople, he knew that should anyone look twice they would peg him as the outsider he was as easily as if he had come wearing his normal three-piece pin-striped suit. His jeans were well worn but not from ranch work, and his boots, which had been broken in walking the streets of Manhattan, didn't show the scarring and scuffing they'd have received in the Pine Nut Mountains and the rock-strewn valleys of this region.

He also knew that should anyone do more than glance his way they would recognize him. He had grown up in this community. These people had been his friends, his neighbors. When he had driven down from Reno earlier that morning and had decided to visit the old ranch before coming into town for the meeting, he had been unprepared for the effect the years of memories would have on him. He was still reeling from the impact. How did the old saying go? You could take a man out of the country, but not the country out of a man? He would have laughed at such sentiment yesterday; today he wasn't so sure.

What fascinated him most was realizing how effectively he had buried his past in his subconscious. Memories he would have had trouble recalling in New York were now as sharp and clear as the edge of a faceted diamond. Warm memories, loving memories . . . and more than a few painful memories. They had inundated him that morning at his old home, flooding him like water from a broken dam.

Opening the door to the ranch house, he had discovered that except for the damage caused by a leaking roof, everything inside was just as he had left it ten years earlier. After his father's long illness and then death, his mother had moved to Lincoln, Nebraska, taking few of the furnishings with her. She had said that leaving everything behind was her way of coping. How like her he must have been, because when he too had left, six months later, he had simply walked out empty-handed, not even locking the door behind him.

Dust and spiderwebs had given the once crisply clean rooms an alien softness, and boards now creaked their protest at the gentlest passage from one room to another. But nothing had prevented Steve from feeling the sharp pain that coursed through him when he eased open the door to the upstairs bedroom and saw the bed that had held his dying father for more than a year. The strong die hard, he thought, for what must have been the hundredth time.

In the quickness of a breath he had again seen his father change from a robust husky man into scarcely a shadow of that man. Steve had stepped from the room and firmly closed the door, unable even after all the years that had passed to accept what had become the final injustice.

So many memories. Cinnamon rolls on Saturday mornings...the excitement of trips into Carson

City... blizzards that made going out to feed the cattle an exercise in survival. Talking Frank Hartman, his best friend, into cutting classes and getting caught by the teacher who'd also skipped school to go fishing.

My God, Frank, how I've missed you, a silent voice inside Steve cried at the powerful and poignant memory of his friend. *You were like the brother I never had...a friend who only comes once in a lifetime. Your life was far too precious a price to pay for such an obscene war....*

Steve ran his hand through his thick black hair. He bent over to pluck a piece of wild grass, then put the stem into his mouth and leaned his back against the rough tree trunk. He wasn't sure just what he had expected to find when he came back; he only knew he had never suspected that, after the passage of so much time, coming home would be so painful.

He had thought he'd said goodbye to his father and to Frank a long time ago. How could he have anticipated the powerful feelings of loss that had come over him at the ranch? Shouldn't ten years have dulled those feelings? At least a little?

He was drawn out of his reverie by a flash of sunlight. For an instant it reflected off a vehicle winding its way down the hillside road, the one he'd just taken into town. His eyes narrowed as he watched the distant speck grow into the distinguishable shape of a truck. His heart began to beat faster. When at last the truck was close enough to make out the double H imprinted on a distinctive beryl-green background, his heart felt as if it would come through his chest. Stepping farther into the shade he anxiously waited for the truck to draw closer. Eagerly he sought a glimpse of the driver.

Danielle Hartman drove by, her eyes fixed straight ahead, wisps of her long brown hair blowing freely about her slender neck. In his mind's eye Steve saw far more than the fleeting glimpse the speeding truck provided. Like photographs from an old album that had been hidden in a sheltered corner of his being, images of the woman who had just passed flashed before him. As clearly as if she stood in front of him, he saw the set of her wide determined jaw, her high sculptured cheekbones that hinted at an Indian heritage somewhere in her western background, her startling blue eyes, as expressive as the spoken word.

He stopped breathing as he watched her pass. Suddenly, with blinding insight, he knew why after staying away for ten long lonely years he had returned.

2

"I'M SORRY, I didn't bring those figures with me to-day, Mrs.... Uh, I'm sorry again. I don't seem to know your name." As if it were written on the papers in front of him, the short thin man with the monk's haircut began to nervously riffle the pages.

"The name is Ms Danielle Hartman, Mr. Berry, and I would like to know why anyone would come to a meeting such as this so obviously unprepared. You've been able to answer only one of my questions and *that* was how to get in touch with Eagle Enterprises." Frustration and anger had made Danielle's voice harsher than she intended, and she knew she was going to lose support of the more conservative ranchers if she didn't tone it down a little. With effort she buried the urge to go after Walt Berry in an unladylike tone and with unladylike language, hiding her irritation behind a wall of politeness.

Slipping her hands into her back pockets to stop their wild wavings, she felt the folded paper she had put there earlier. Written on that paper were the statistics she'd brought to counter any claims Eagle Enterprises might make of minimal water usage. But the statistics were useless if she couldn't get him to make any claims for her to counter. She was grateful she had at last managed to keep her temper under enough control so as not to blurt out the information she had worked so hard to gather. That would have given him the opportunity to go back to Reno to play with the figures until they came out sounding reasonable.

"Well, frankly, Ms Hartman," the man said, his smile weakening at the corners, "I did not anticipate any questions about water today. Let me reassure you, however, that studies have been done and are available for—"

"Where can I get one?" Purposely she softened her tone to one of willing cooperation.

"Why, uh...I'll have to check on that for you." His hand passed quickly over his bald pate.

This time Danielle felt better about the murmuring she heard around her. "Please do that, Mr. Berry," she said politely as she sat back down on the cushion-covered pew.

She watched him respond to the spate of questions on water that her own querying had aroused, wondering how much of his nervousness was attributable to his unorthodox surroundings and how much was just pure ineptness. She had anticipated a formidable opponent; finding someone pathetically weak was a little unnerving. If the guns Eagle Enterprises had prepared to fire were no more powerful than these, perhaps there was a chance she could win the battle after all.

At the swell of hope she hadn't allowed herself to feel before now she surreptitiously crossed long work-roughened fingers on both hands. The day seemed much brighter than it had when she had stopped at the Maddox ranch.

But then Jack Gibson, Weberstown's mayor, walked down the narrow aisle and up to the pulpit. In a demonstration of affection that made Danielle clench her teeth he put his arm lightly around Walt Berry's shoulders. Then he looked at the townspeople and ranchers gathered there and said, "Well, folks, it seems that we may have come on a little too strong today. It was unfair of us not to give Mr. Berry here more time to prepare for this kind of questioning." He paused a moment to grin at Berry and pat him on the back.

"Of course we all understand Danielle Hartman's concern that this be handled properly," he went on. "After all, the Maddox place is right next door to hers." He looked directly at her. "But I personally want to reassure you, Danielle, that all of us here in Weberstown—even though I admit we won't be able to actually see the new casino from the town—we are still every bit as concerned as you are that things be handled right and proper. I want you to know that every one of us here in town will continue to look out for you through this thing—just like we've all looked out for you since your momma and daddy died."

You bastard! Danielle seethed, meeting his grinning certitude with a fiery glare. Slowly she stood. She answered him with deceptive calm. "I certainly appreciate your reassurances, Mr. Mayor, but I feel I should reiterate that it isn't only the immediate consequences of the project that concern me—or whether or not, as you so succinctly put it, 'I'm being looked out for.' What I'm concerned about, as we all should be, are the subtle, hidden ramifications of allowing a business—which would eventually draw upward of ten thousand people—to be built in our ecologically balanced community."

There was a momentary distraction as someone quietly opened the door and a harsh shaft of sunlight brightened the interior of the church. Danielle went on, refusing to be sidetracked by the interruption. "I don't know whether or not you've played with those figures on your computer, *John* but just in case you haven't, that averages out to be almost ten new people for every one now living in our two valleys." She glanced at the people seated around her. "Are we really willing to forever abandon this life as we know it just for a possible handful of gold?"

John Gibson frowned. "Please refrain from making any more speeches, Danielle. We've all been privy to your fireball rhetoric a hundred times already."

Quit while you're ahead, Danielle. Don't let him get to you. She took a deep calming breath. "I couldn't agree with you more, Mr. Mayor. What we need now are facts and figures if we are to vote intelligently on this. Perhaps Mr. Berry could be talked into going back to Reno and spending some time preparing those facts and figures and then returning in the near future." Loud clapping from the audience followed her suggestion.

"Ah, now I really don't think it's necessary to ask Walt here to drive all the way back to Weberstown. I'm sure he could just send the information and we could go over it at the next council meeting."

Danielle started to protest, but her words were cut off by a loud objection from someone in the front row. Several informal shouts of agreement accompanied the objection.

Walt Berry held up his hands, motioning for quiet. "I would be happy to gather whatever information you request and return as soon as I have it."

The meeting was formally ended with John Gibson's expansive promise to let everyone know when the next meeting would be. Anxious to get back to work, the people abandoned the tiny church with very little of the casual visiting that would have taken place if it had been a Sunday. Soon only Danielle and the grizzled owner of the town's blacksmith shop remained behind. The old fellow had indicated that he wanted to speak to her.

He waited for the last person out to close the door before he spoke, "I just wanted you to know that I'm in your corner," he said, reaching out to touch her arm with a hand twisted and gnarled by years of working at an anvil. "Don't let that pompous ass, Gibson, get you down or make you give up on what you think is right. I don't speak up myself about all this 'cause I know they ain't none of them gonna to listen to me. But I didn't want you to think I wasn't with you." He released her arm. "That's all I had to tell you. I'll be going now." He turned and headed down the aisle. When he reached the door, he turned and winked. "Your dad would've been real proud of how you stood up to 'em."

Danielle smiled and waved goodbye. When the door had closed again she turned to pick up her hat. Her earlier elation had begun to fade, leaving room for a niggling fear that all was not as simple as it seemed. Even from the little she had been able to learn at the library about Eagle Enterprises, it just didn't make sense that the corporation would send someone like Walt Berry to conduct its business . . . unless Berry didn't play the game by the normal rules and had constructed an elaborate ruse of incompetence to lull the opposition. How in the world was she going to find out whether his ineptitude was real or only a brilliant act?

Lost in her thoughts as she moved toward the door, Danielle was not immediately aware of the movement in the darkened alcove at the side of the big double doors. And then she had a sudden, overwhelming feeling of no longer being alone. She glanced around as she put her hand on the brass doorknob.

She saw him at once. And just as quickly she felt the thundering of her heart and a tightness in her chest that made her struggle to catch a breath.

It was as if she had seen him yesterday and yet...he was not the same. His hair was still the thick black curling mass she had remembered, and it still brushed stubbornly across his forehead, but now he wore it shorter than the rebellious young man he had been when he had left. His boyish leanness was gone. In its place was a man's body—filled out, gracefully molded, well cared for. Yet ... despite the solid width of his shoulders, Danielle was sure he would feel the same as she so painfully and so frustratingly remembered on long lonely nights.

Her gaze went to his arms, where the cuffs of his shirt had been carelessly rolled back. Inconsequently she noted that his skin wasn't as dark as it had once been. She wondered if it was because he no longer worked outside. Somehow she hadn't pictured him making his living behind a desk. Her dreams of him were always inexplicably melded with the openness of the outdoors. Never had she imagined that he would choose to spend his life differently.

For long seconds they stared, neither speaking, but both absorbing the sight of each other as if they had been told it would be their last chance. Finally Steve broke the crushing silence that had begun to grow like an ever widening chasm between them.

"How are you, Danny?" he asked softly.

Such a simple question. How should she answer? *I'm fine, Steve. How are you?* or, *I'm finally beginning to get along all right now. After all, ten years is plenty of time to get over someone you once loved, don't you think?*

"I'm the same as I've always been, Steve. But then, didn't you tell me when you left that small-town people never change?" She hadn't meant for it to sound so biting, so bitter.

In the softly caressing tone she remembered so well, he replied, "I said a lot of things when I left."

"Yes..." she said slowly, reluctantly, as if afraid that by giving an inch of the hillside she had built to defend herself she would tumble the mile to the bottom. "I guess we both did."

Steve watched her, aching to touch her with a craving that was an actual physical pain, yet unable to move. So much had passed between them; he had no right to intrude in her life again. But to hell with rights. It had been so long since he had felt the silkiness of her glistening hair as it passed through his fingers . . . so long since he had made love to a woman whom he also loved.

But what he saw reflected in her eyes was not the welcome he would have wished. Desperately trying to bring the conversation back to more neutral ground, where they might find a way to communicate at least on a friendly level, he asked, "How are your folks?"

A tiny frown created fine lines in the deeply tanned flesh between her brows. "They were killed in an automobile accident almost three years ago," she answered evenly, without emotion.

"I'm sorry. I didn't know."

How could he have known? Just as he had lived frozen in time in her memory, so would her parents have lived in his. She sighed heavily and glanced out the single clear pane of the small stained-glass window next to the door.

Steve crossed the short distance that still separated them so that he stood beside her. He came so close he needed only to raise his hand and he would have touched her. Still they remained apart, the barriers between them too solid to be breached even by another shared tragedy.

"I wish I had known," he said with a helpless shrug.

Her eyes filled with a sudden fire. "Why? What would you have done?" As quickly as she spoke the words she wished she could call them back.

So soon after seeing each other again they were separated as dramatically and as forcefully as lightning cuts through the space between two electrically charged clouds. Her long-held, intensely private dream that they might someday, somehow, come together was nothing more than a dream. Too many bad memories kept them apart. Too many sorrows. Inwardly Danielle cursed the reality of the destruction of that dream with the vehemence a man dying of thirst would curse the mirage he thought was an oasis.

Steve's hand reached toward her, then dropped back to his side. "I would have tried to help—"

"What you really mean is that you would have flown in and graced me with your presence for a week or two of hand holding, then you would have disappeared again."

"No, Danny, that's not what I meant." He answered her attack so softly that his voice was little more than a calming whisper. "I would have tried to help you with all the mundane things you had to face, in the hope that it would make the hurt a little less. Perhaps I might have helped with all the paperwork that seems to demand immediate attention when someone dies, or I could have helped to run the ranch while you did the paperwork yourself.... I don't know what I might have done, I only meant that I would have tried to give back some of what you gave me when I lost dad."

Because she needed something to do with her hands, she reached up to tuck a tendril of hair behind her ear. "It's really a moot point, isn't it, Steve? If you recall, when you left Nevada it was with deliberate finality. You told me that nothing would ever bring you back here. I simply took you at your word."

"You knew I would come if you needed me."

She stared at him. Long seconds passed as she tried to control the emotions that tore at her like the wind tears at a tree of autumn leaves. "I needed you when you left...."

There it was. Spoken aloud for the first time. Something she had never before admitted because her pride had not permitted it.

He met her gaze with one as strong and unyielding as her own. "No more than I needed you to leave with me, Danny."

And once again, as if it had been yesterday instead of ten years ago, their parting and the pain it had created stood between them.

"Do you think we'll ever resolve it, Danny? Will we ever decide whose need was greater?"

"No." The word was little more than a sigh. "And even if we did—" she forced a smile of resignation "—what good would it do now?"

Danielle shifted her weight to her other foot, retreating slightly from Steve's pervasive presence. "It looks like we'll never change, Steve. I can still remember your dad breaking up one of our more vocal arguments by telling us that if stubbornness were a commodity, we would both be incredibly rich someday." She glanced at his clothes and then at her own. "It seems that neither of us have found any buyers."

His answering smile took her completely by surprise. How could she have forgotten his beautiful smile—the magic that it wove around her heart...the grip it still held her in.

But then their last years together had been filled with such tragedy that there had been little occasion for laughter. Conjuring up an image of him deep in grief or lost in the passion of their burgeoning love was as easy as closing her eyes, but to find laughter meant going back to their childhood. Going back to the years Steve and her brother Frank had spent together, rattling through each other's homes with all the confident exuberance of teenage boys in the unconscious process of putting together a friendship that would have lasted a lifetime. Going back to the years before Vietnam.

Danielle couldn't remember a time when she hadn't loved Steve Maddox. Even when she had been ignored or barely tolerated or simply considered "Frank's pesky little sister," she had held a special corner of her heart in reserve for him. Not until she was seventeen and had provided a soft and willing shoulder for him to lean on in his grief had he seen her as a woman; it had been a long frustrating year before he had broken through the final barriers that separated them and they had become lovers. And another year and a half for them to complete the building of a love so intense that she had become a shattered empty shell when he'd left.

They had had so little time. Was it any wonder she had spent the past ten years longing for more?

With a teasing smile he reached over to tuck back the wisp of hair that had worked its way loose again. "You would never make disparaging remarks about my clothing if you knew how carefully I dressed this morning."

His words and his unanticipated touch brought her back from her musings with a snap. Suddenly the reason for her being in Weberstown on a morning when there were a dozen pressing things to do on the ranch came back with a throat-tightening force. "Why are you here?" she asked, deeply afraid of his answer.

He hesitated only an instant, but it was long enough to send a cold chill down Danielle's spine. How stupid she had been to become so wrapped up in seeing him again that she hadn't thought to wonder at his abrupt appearance. An overwhelming sense of impending doom settled over her, blanketing her shoulders like a cloak. She fought an urge to press her fingers to his lips to stop his reply. She wanted only a little more time with him . . . just a little more.

Liar! What she really wanted was a lifetime. . . .

Steve raked his hand through his hair, forcing back the errant wave that dipped across his forehead. He started to speak, then turned and began to walk back and forth across the tiny space between the door and alcove. To start an unconscious nervous pacing when he had something bad to relay was another thing about Steve that obviously hadn't changed. It was the worst thing he could have done for Danielle's fledgling hope that her fears were groundless.

Stopping in front of her again he reached for her hand, but she moved away, knowing what physical contact with him would do to her sensibilities.

"I prepared a dozen answers for that question," he said slowly. "At least one for every possible circumstance and person I could imagine. Only I forgot someone—you." Again his hand raked through his hair.

"No...not forgot, just hid somewhere in my mind," he continued. His forehead furrowed in puzzlement. "I must have realized you would still be in Weberstown, at least subconsciously. But I guess I must have somehow managed to convince myself that seeing you again wouldn't bother me any more than seeing anyone else."

"And?"

Even as he struggled he knew he would never be able to find the words to tell her what seeing her again had done to him. How could he express what his life had been like without her? "And I was wrong," he finally, simply, said.

"You still haven't answered me, Steve. Why did you come back?"

"Couldn't we talk about it later?"

He was giving her an alternative, a way that they *could* have more time together. Her mind screamed that she tell him yes, that it could indeed wait. "I think we should talk about it now."

He sighed wearily. "I'm here because of the casino."

Confusion shone from her eyes. "Are you telling me that you still own the ranch?"

"Yes."

Danielle thought for a minute, her hand lightly massaging her forehead. "But we were all told that Eagle Enterprises...." She jerked her head up so that their gazes met. "*You're* Eagle Enterprises?"

He nodded slowly.

"*You're* behind this whole thing? This . . . this rape of my valley? My ranch? My life?"

To control the urge to reach for her he shoved his hands in his back pockets. His shoulders squared as his stance subtly changed to a defensive position. "I planned to put a piece of unproductive land to profitable use—that's all. No rape. No insidious, devious motivations."

"You'll never be able to convince me of that." She was surprised that her voice didn't betray her rage. "You planned this as some kind of perverted revenge—some obscene way to pay me back for choosing to stay here instead of going with you ten years ago." Somehow she still managed to speak in a controlled even tone.

"You can't possibly believe that."

"I'll tell you what I can believe. I can't believe that any of this is happening. I can't believe that you're involved in something so terrible . . . so vindictive." A catch in her throat made her voice quaver slightly, and she knew her battle to remain outwardly calm was lost.

"I—"

"Don't try to tell me it never occurred to you how I would feel about what you planned to do. That you wouldn't know what it would do to me when I found out that you were behind this whole thing." The hurt she felt ran so deeply and cut so sharply that she wished with all her heart a big black hole would open up and pull her into its cool unfeeling depths.

"I'm not trying to tell you anything except the truth. Finding land or companies that aren't living up to their potential and turning them around to become profit-making projects is what I happen to do for a living."

"No matter who or what happens to be in your way, I suppose."

"Who am I hurting, Danny? How is bringing some civilization to this backward little section of Nevada going to hurt its citizens?"

"Backward! How in hell would someone who hasn't spent ten minutes in ten years in a community know how backward it is?"

"I'm sorry. My choice of words was inexcusably poor."

"Poor, maybe. But they were plainly indicative of the feelings behind the person using them. You've obviously forgotten that we country people *choose* to live the way we do. We aren't bound to this kind of life by some giant invisible chain. The road that leads to the big city lets us travel on it, too, you know. If we wanted that kind of life we would go after it. But you tell me—where do we go when, because of the consummate greed on a few people's part, the life we happen to reject comes to us?"

Softly he asked, "Are you absolutely sure that there is a 'we'?"

"What you really mean is am I alone in not wanting the casino built?"

"Are you?"

He had found her weak spot. "Apathy doesn't nec-essarily mean acquiescence," she said. "I don't think most of these people have looked past the 'pie in the sky' your report promised." Her voice took on a deeply cutting edge. "Especially since one of your biggest selling points was that the casino would be tucked back into the far corner of Star Valley—not visible or in the least intrusive to the people in town, only bothersome to one medium-sized, inconse-quential ranch that just happens to be right next door. But then, the casino wouldn't affect the actual run-ning of that ranch—only the esthetics. How amaz-ingly selfish of me to try to prevent such an unexpected windfall to be bestowed on our 'back-ward' little community."

He studied her for long seconds before answering. "Is there anything I could say or do that would con-vince you none of this was done to hurt you?"

"Nothing."

"I thought as much."

Why was it suddenly so hard for her to breathe?

"It seems there's nothing more for us to say to each other," he said.

But surely there was. How could the dream of see-ing him again—the dream that had been like a lifeline supporting her through all of those long lonely years—how could it die so easily? And on such an or-dinary morning.

"No, I guess not," she answered tonelessly. With-out even the backward glance she ached to cast, she left the church and walked the short distance to her truck.

Before opening the door she turned and faced him again. He was standing on the porch watching her, his eyes hooded, noncommittal. Seeing him there, she allowed herself to feel for an instant just how desperately she had wanted him to reach out and touch her. A pain shot through her chest.

With forced determination she raised her chin. "I'll fight you on this, Steve."

When she saw that he wasn't going to answer she climbed into the truck and drove away.

Steve watched her until the truck was no more than a speck traveling along the hillside road toward Star Valley. His mind was in turmoil, his emotions disjointed, conflicting. Only one thought surfaced clear and bright and sparkling—he would not let her go this time. He would not lose her again.

3

DANIELLE HAD TRAVELED less than half a mile into Star Valley when she had to stop the truck at the side of the road because she could no longer see. She slumped against the steering wheel as great heaving sobs racked her body.

It wasn't so much that her dream had been shattered into pieces, impossible to reconstruct. It was knowing that her reason for facing each new day with the hope that perhaps it was the day she would see Steve again was gone.

For years she had fought knowing or admitting it, but finally, after a disastrous six-month marriage, she had been forced to come to terms with the knowledge that Steve was so deeply ingrained in the fiber that made her the person she was that there was simply no room for anyone else.

Until he had come back, she had been able to fantasize that he would return to her again as a knight on a white horse might—to sweep her away in his loving arms, carrying her off....

Her palms dug into her eyes. It was a fairy tale that someone almost thirty years old had no right having.

It was about time that she faced reality, no matter how painful or stark that reality happened to be.

Still, it was so hard to give up a dream . . . so hard to let go.

Danielle propped her chin on her arms and looked over the wide arc of the leather-covered steering wheel. Stretched out before her was her beloved Star Valley: sagebrush, sand and wild grasses, with a year-round river running through the center. Rimmed on three sides by spectacular mountains and on the fourth by gently rolling hills. Her home.

She knew every nuance of this country. There wasn't an arroyo that didn't spark a memory. And always those memories led back to Steve. When she was a gangly young girl, Frank had been the catalyst who had brought them together. Frank, the perfect older brother, incredibly tolerant of a tag-along sister who was sometimes forced on him—a sister about as wanted at that age in a boy's life as a wart on the end of his nose. And wherever Frank had gone he was eventually joined by Steve.

Danielle couldn't remember when Steve hadn't made her heart quicken. From the time she had been barely old enough to go to school and had watched a Steve still in his preteens struggle to load a bale of hay onto the back of a pickup to the time she'd watched the boy grown to man lift the sixty-pound bundles as if they were hollow—through all those years she had known she loved him.

It had been the driving force of a girl impatient to become a woman. How desperately she had tried to make him love her in return. In her twelfth year she had developed into a long-legged, flat-chested, transitional female who wore braces and stumbled over her own shadow. That summer she had spent hours in her room, agonizing over the certainty she would never be the woman destined to capture Steve Maddox's heart. And then, as if to give validity to her fears, Steve and Frank had started double-dating, sometimes bringing their older worldlier girlfriends to the house.

Her parents had never connected her dramatic weekend crying sessions to Steve, or if they had, they were kind enough not to mention it. But Danielle could still hear her mother telling her father, "Leave her alone, Adam. It's part of the growing-up process we women go through."

Vignettes for a stormy winter night in front of a fireplace. Stories to warm, to comfort, to bring a smile. Certainly nothing to cause the pain she now suffered. No, those images came later.

Danielle's gaze swung to the west and the softly mounded hills at the foot of the Pine Nut Mountains, and for a time she indulged herself, letting herself sink back into the joy that had been hers on a very special day more than eleven years earlier.

She had had a free morning and had offered to help Steve bring a herd of cattle down from the high range that backed onto his ranch. When she had driven up to the Maddox barn, Steve had been in the process of loading the horses onto the trailer. The predawn of late autumn was crisp and cold, without a hint of the warmth the sun would later bring. Danielle had rubbed her arms as she waited for Steve to finish.

"I thought maybe you'd changed your mind," he said, slapping the rump of the roan he had just led into the trailer.

"I decided that before I left I'd better check on that group of calves we've been having trouble with."

"Haven't you heard anything from the vet? I thought the lab work was due back yesterday."

"It was, but it still hasn't come in. Dad's getting pretty worried. We lost two more last night."

Steve slipped his arm familiarly across Danielle's shoulders as he walked around the truck. "It doesn't make sense. I haven't seen a sign of it in any of my calves."

She was acutely aware of his sleeve brushing the back of her neck, of the clean fresh smell of his flannel shirt and the softer, more elusive aroma of the soap he had used the night before. Whenever he spontaneously touched her she felt as if an internal button had been pushed, one that immediately sent a signal to all of her senses. She seemed to become so acutely aware of every part of him that his nearness sometimes bordered on being painful. If only the motivation behind his actions were not those of brother to sister.

Since Frank's death, her own life and the way other people treated her had changed dramatically. Her parents had at first reluctantly and then purposely thrust her into Frank's role, subtly letting her know in a hundred different ways that the continuation of the Double H Ranch by the Hartman family now rested solely on her shoulders.

Sometime during that year Steve had finally noticed her as a woman—but he still related to her as Frank's sister. He had tried to become the brother she no longer had, when what she really wanted him to be was her lover. It was to her constant frustration that she lacked the wiles or the sophistication to make him see her as she really was.

He opened the truck door for her, and as she climbed inside he slapped her on the rump with the same degree of personal involvement he had shown the horse earlier. It was the final culminating bit of evidence that if she didn't do something brash and do it soon, she would never be able to break the mold he seemed intent on forcing her into.

When Steve was seated beside her and they were on their way to the mountains, she turned to look at him in the dim light of the cab.

"Is something wrong?" he asked, finally noticing her staring at him.

"Nothing out of the ordinary," she answered meaningfully. And then to herself, *But something that isn't going beyond today.*

He looked at her, his eyebrows raised in silent question.

"You'll find out," she promised mysteriously.

Later that day, when they stopped to rest their horses and to get themselves something to eat, Danielle realized that deciding to do something was far easier than actually doing it. Twice she had had the words she wanted to say on the tip of her tongue, ready to tumble out at the gentlest shove, yet she'd been unable to begin the sentence.

Somehow, Steve, I think it's about time we stopped fooling around and started developing a more intimate relationship, or *Steve, I've been in love with you since the first day I saw you, so would you please love me back?* seemed incredibly bold and excessively aggressive...and worst of all, doomed to failure. For all her resolve she was no closer to what she wanted than before she'd made her impassioned promise to herself. *Coward!* she inwardly seethed.

Disgustedly she leaned back on the blanket Steve had brought for them and closed her eyes against the bleached blue sky.

After she had been there several minutes a low chuckle made her eyes snap open. Steve, who was sitting on a low flat rock across from her, tossed a dried seed pod in her direction. "How about letting me in on what's going on in that head of yours?"

She stared at him, a puzzled look in her eyes.

"I've never seen anyone go through so many different facial expressions in such a short period of time in my entire life," he explained.

She sat up. "You mean in all of the amazingly long twenty-three years of it?"

"Twenty-three years and four months."

"Forgive me. I keep forgetting what an old man you are."

Suddenly serious, he said, "Age isn't what made me an old man, Danny."

She stared into his eyes, wishing she knew a way to heal the hurt she saw there. "Why don't you ever talk to me about what happened in Vietnam? Maybe it would help you to put it behind you."

Steve stuck a golden piece of wild grass in his mouth and held it there, thoughtfully chewing the sweetness before answering. "Some things aren't helped by talking about them. Besides, they aren't the kinds of things that I would want you to know about."

"Why? What makes me so special?"

"Because you're who you are. Like it or not, Danny, you're different from most people. You've been insulated from a lot of things because you've lived in this valley all of your life—" he took the grass from his mouth "—just as Frank and I had. We were all raised to believe in the basic goodness of man. It's hard to discover that it's not always the way things are."

It was the most Steve had said about Vietnam since he'd returned. Danielle felt as if they had been surrounded by something special, and that if she moved too quickly or spoke too loudly the moment would disappear.

"Steve," she began softly, pleadingly. "Look at me. Look past the image you have created in your mind and see who I really am. I'm tougher than you think. I'm more of a woman than you realize. You treat me precisely the way Frank used to. But I am not your sister. I never will be. I don't want to be. If you could look beyond the person you think I should be to the person I am, you would realize how desperately I reject the role you have created for me. . . ." And then so softly she wasn't sure if she was still speaking aloud, she added, "And how desperately I want you to love me as a man loves a woman."

He smiled then. To smile at the most unexpected times was a trait of his she had never understood and doubted she ever would. But it was a trait she found far more endearing than disconcerting.

"It's certainly taken you long enough," he finally said.

She was too surprised to do anything but mutter an almost incomprehensible, "Wh-what are you s-sa-saying?"

"I've been aware of you as a woman for a long time now, Danny. Almost a year."

"Why didn't you say something?"

"I was waiting for you," he answered.

Her shoulders sagged. This was not going the way she had envisioned at all. The moment she had dreamed about and planned a dozen different ways grew into an uncomfortable silence. She studied the desert floor between her outstretched jean-clad legs. When finally she had summoned enough nerve to glance up and see if he was looking at her, she found him studying her with an amused look in his eyes. Instantly anger shot through her. "Always in charge, aren't you? Okay, Mr. Know-It-All, now what do we do?"

Steve had slipped from his rock and come over to kneel in front of her. Gone was the playful gleam that had been in his eyes, replaced by a dusky look of passion. He reached up to touch her face, letting his fingers slowly follow the contour of her high cheekbones and widely determined jaw.

"This may prove to be impossible for us to do," he said gently. "Like it or not, our relationship has been radically different up to this moment. I want you to tell me if—"

She started to protest, to tell him how often they had already breached the barriers of friendship in her dreams, but realized in a flush of shyness that he was right. He took her hand in his and slowly brought it to his mouth. For the first time she felt the touch of his lips against her flesh. She watched his face, her own becoming suffused with a passion still innocent. When he touched her palm with the tip of his tongue, she felt a fire race from her hand to a place deep in her loins.

"Danny?" Steve said softly, his voice filled with concern. "What's wrong?"

She gave her head a tiny shake. "Nothing...."

"Are you sure?" he asked.

This time she nodded, her mouth too dry for anything as mundane as words.

"Then unbend a little ... touch me," he encouraged.

Touch him? Where should she touch him? How? Frantically she sought a modicum of the sophisticated lover she always was in her dreams. As the seconds passed by in a cruel mimicry of hours, she saw an understanding warmth come to Steve's eyes. Gently he chided her, "I only meant for you to put your arms around me, Danny. That's all ... nothing more."

His hand went to her neck; his fingers touched the soft hair at her nape; his thumb stroked her jaw. "The rest will come ..." With barely perceptible pressure he urged her toward him. "Maybe not today...if not, then another." Closer and closer they came together. "If this loving is meant to be between us, the rest will come to you as naturally as the stars to a midnight sky." Their lips touched. The contact was so light she wondered if it had happened only in her imagination. He lingered, letting her breath caress him, waiting for her to complete the kiss. With a soft moan she reached up to wrap her arms around his neck.

His mouth had been wonderfully soft and welcoming. Fires long banked by innocence had sparked to life as if fueled by strips of the finest dried kindling. Swept up in the building firestorm, Danielle had stopped reacting to Steve with conscious thought. Her responses had slipped to a level of instinct. Her lips parted in invitation; her tongue tasted in tiny arousing thrusts. She had learned the thrilling eloquence of a sigh, the depth of meaning in a restrained groan of pleasure....

Danielle sat up in the truck as if she had been struck. She caught her breath at the sharp pain that sliced through her chest. The memory of their lovemaking was so clear—almost tangible. What they had once shared seemed so enticingly close yet so cruelly distant. She blinked back the fresh tears of pain and frustration that threatened to spill over her lashes. Though she knew how futile it was to do so, she let her mind slip back once more to the memory, the proverbial moth returning to the flame.

She felt again how intensely she had felt a loss when he'd left her to make a bed for them on the sand. How thoughtfully slow he had been as he helped her to take off her clothes. As each garment was removed he had silently sought confirmation that she had not changed her mind, letting her know that if she had, it was all right. Finally her reassurances had taken the form of boldness in her role of lover. She had purposely sought the places on his lean frame she thought would bring him pleasure. After only a few such reassurances he had lost the fear that she might later regret what they were doing, and he had treated her as a partner in their lovemaking....

Shutting her eyes tightly and leaning her head against the back of the seat, Danielle bit her lip to keep from crying out. She held herself tightly, caught up in the nearly overwhelming sensations the erotic memories of that special time had again engulfed her in. Her breasts ached at his remembered touch; her lips were bereft, the desire to feel his pressed against them overwhelming. And he had come back. He'd once again been close enough for her to reach out and touch. If only....

Angry at her turn of thoughts, Danielle glanced down at the dashboard clock. She had wasted more than forty-five minutes on an incredibly self-indulgent futile lapse into melancholia—as if such thoughts would make any difference in what she must do, or the outcome. There was no other way to proceed but to give up even the remnants of her shattered dream. No matter how hard it would be for her to let go, let go she would.

Searching through the clutter in the glove box she found a napkin that had been left over from her last visit to a fast-food restaurant in Reno. She used the scratchy paper to wipe her eyes and blow her nose before stuffing it into the ashtray.

Taking a deep calming breath, she pulled back onto the road. Unconsciously she clamped her jaw in newfound determination. Her tears were spent. She had used up all the time she would allow herself for sorrow over what might have been. So many years had already been wasted. From now on, all of her energy would be focused on keeping Steve Maddox and Eagle Enterprises from ruining Star Valley. And from now on she would ruthlessly avoid erotic daydreams of what once had been.

Somehow, some way, she would win. She would keep at least one thing she loved—her land—as it had always been. After today she would leave fairy tales and their cloying happy endings to children.

As she drove along the bumpy road to the ranch she forced herself to concentrate on the job she had chosen to do. She might not have the knowledge or cunning equal to what Steve would be able to muster against her, but she had toughness and tenacity—and the instincts of a survivor. Surely someone who had lived her entire life—someone who made her living—in an environment as unforgiving as the Nevada desert was a worthy adversary for someone who had gone soft sitting behind a desk pushing a pencil, as Steve obviously now did. Somewhere in a quiet corner of her mind she heard a voice saying that Steve no more looked like the picture she had just painted of him than a bull looked like a cow.

Danielle was still involved in her personal pep talk when she drove up to the barn and parked beside the mower, making sure she stopped where the afternoon shade would make the truck cab habitable in case she had to drive somewhere else that day. She looked up to see Ben Reed, a welcome apparition, making his way through the lingering cloud of dust she had created.

Ben Reed was her foreman, her right-hand man, her father, her brother, her friend—he embodied all the male role models she now lacked in her life, save one. He had been an integral part of the Double H Ranch since before her birth, someone she had always run to with a scraped knee or a bruised heart before she would run to her own father. With his normal stoical and accepting calm—a calm that to Danielle always seemed like the hushed aftermath of a violent storm—Ben had seen her through Steve and later through her calamitous marriage. He had seen her through the years when her parents, grieving for their son, had placed more and more responsibility for the ranch on her shoulders. Taciturn with others, he was open and giving of himself with her.

Threaded through the memories of her childhood like the third piece of a braid were the lazy evenings at the ranch when the day's work was done. Ben would welcome the little girl onto the porch of his house, and after her bit of coaxing he would regale her with yet another of the stories his father had told him about the West the way it used to be. More than any-one else, Ben had instilled in her a love for the land and a sense of oneness with it. That sense of oneness, had helped to see Danielle through the blackest depths of her personal tragedies.

Now a virile fifty-eight-year-old bachelor, Ben had a woman friend in Carson City who had been keeping him company for more than six years.

Passing Danielle with a curt nod of recognition and a "Howdy, Missy," he walked around the truck and opened the passenger door. Reaching under the seat he withdrew the tire iron and muttered, "Damn!" As he slammed the door Danielle heard him chorus a familiar lament. "If people would just put things back where they got 'em...."

"What is it this time?"

"The pipe wrench's missing."

"Why do you need the pipe wrench?" she asked, already knowing the answer. "I thought you were going to start vaccinating the herd on the east range today."

Ben leaned against the side of the truck, his elbows supporting his lanky torso. "I am if I can ever get to it. But first I have to find that damn wrench. Russ needs to fix that sprinkler we've been having trouble with up on the high pasture. It finally totally gave way this morning."

She frowned. "Haven't the new parts come in yet?"

"I called Wilkie's Hardware and they said they're still waiting on the factory to get the washers to them. Russ is just going to have to Band-Aid it again till they get here." Suddenly, as if really seeing her for the first time, his expression reflected a different concern. "What's your problem, Danny? You look like someone just kicked your dog."

As usual he had ignored the formalities. "You mean all mad and sad at the same time?" She tried to smile.

"Something like that."

To avoid his intense gaze she looked down at her dust-covered boots. There was no sense putting it off. Tonelessly she said, "Steve's back."

The meaningful silence that followed was incredibly painful. She knew what thoughts were going through Ben's mind. She knew he would assume the best, and she hated having to tell him that the reason Steve had returned after being away so long was not because he had suddenly discovered he could no longer live without her.

"The reason he's come back has something to do with this casino thing, doesn't it?" Ben asked.

Danielle's head snapped up. "How did you know?"

"It wasn't that hard to figure. I got to thinking a while back that we never really heard that the land had been sold. We only guessed it had." He rubbed his chin, his hand brushing the ends of his bushy mustache. "I'm only surprised it took so long. Land with water, even land that's over an hour away from the city, brings in a nice pocketful of change. It'd be stupid for Steve to let it just set. I only wish he'd've gotten in touch with us when he finally decided he wanted to do something with it instead of selling out to that Eagle Enterprises outfit."

"Steve Maddox is Eagle Enterprises."

He whistled softly. "No kidding." Again his hand rubbed across his chin. "Well, that sure makes those last few pieces of the puzzle slip in real smooth and easy like. Now that it's all come together, it sure seems odd we were so slow seeing it before. It sure fits."

"Yeah, like a cheap pair of jeans."

"Was the run-in between you two that bad then?"

Danielle flinched. "If you don't mind, I'd rather not go into the details."

He started to answer, then stopped and began again as if he had changed his mind about what he wanted to say. "What are you going to do?"

"I'll do whatever I need to do to stop him."

"That's the kind of line that sounds real good in Western movies, Danny, but unless you've got a scriptwriter working on your side, you'd better come up with something a little better. And real soon."

"Good lines I can come up with. Good ideas don't come as easily."

"What kind of reaction did you get on the water usage?"

"I never had a chance to use it."

Again the hand rubbed his chin. "Have you thought to check if a preliminary petition for re-zoning has been filed?"

Danielle slapped her forehead with the palm of her hand. "No!" she groaned.

"It's only a shot in the dark. But if things haven't gone too far, you might be able to stop him there."

"I'll try anything."

He grinned. "Let me know what you find out. Maybe we can put our heads together and come up with something workable."

"The way I've been operating lately I can't help but think we'll wind up with one-and-a-half minds," she replied, disgust evident in her words and tone. "I'll let you know the minute I get back."

After checking with Russell Edwards, the only other employee who, with his family, lived year round at the ranch, to see if he needed anything in town, Danielle was once again behind the wheel of her truck. She turned off the gravel road onto the public strip of asphalt that served as the connecting link between Weberstown and the Carson City highway, and had gone less than a mile when she made a U turn.

What she wanted to accomplish was far too important to entrust to the inexpert naive hands of someone who hadn't even thought to check if a rezoning petition had been filed. If there was any hope at all of winning, she needed someone who knew what he was doing. That meant going into Reno and talking to Roger McIntosh, her ranch lawyer. Once there she would call Ben and let him know that she couldn't be home as early as anticipated.

Almost two hours later she was standing on the sidewalk outside her lawyer's office, seething with frustration. Normally a precise methodical person, she had driven all the way into Reno without even bothering to call to see if McIntosh would be in. And, of course, he wasn't. Now she had to decide whether or not to stay the night and see him first thing in the morning or drive back home and make another round trip from the ranch tomorrow.

It was no contest. She couldn't remember the last time she had felt as exhausted this early in the day. A long bath and a night's rest sounded as good as a two-month vacation—another thing she kept promising herself she would do someday.

She stopped at a phone booth to make a reservation at the hotel where she and Ben always stayed when either of them were in town, went by the bank to get money from the instant-teller machine and stopped by a drugstore for the few personal things she would need for her meeting the next day. In a moment of pure self-indulgence she pulled into the aisle reserved for valet parking and turned her keys over to a young man who didn't look old enough to shave, let alone drive. Wearily she brushed her hair back from her face, and as if in a trance, walked into the Golden Door Casino and Hotel.

Deep burgundy carpeting with a raucous green pattern running through it, huge crystal chandeliers, gleaming brass railings and dark polished walnut desks and paneling combined to make the lobby of the hotel a classic example of overstated opulence. Tacky was usually the first word that came to Danielle's mind whenever she entered the place, and garish followed a close second. If it hadn't been for the deference the hotel staff paid to Nevada's ranchers, and the same staff's willingness to find room for them when every other hotel in town claimed to be booked solid, she would have switched to something more subdued.

But tonight as she registered, she scarcely noticed the lobby decor. She was at the part of the registration form that asked for her license number when she heard a voice behind her—a voice that made her feel as if she had suddenly been thrust into a snow-fed mountain stream.

"By any chance are you looking for me?"

Before he had appeared she had heard the cacophony of the adjoining casino; now she heard only the timbre of his voice. Slowly she turned around, expecting to find a mocking smile on Steve Maddox's face. Instead she found a look that made her bite back the sarcastic retort teetering on the end of her tongue.

His eyes reflected the trusting hope and promise of a child's on Christmas morning. Searching for something to say, she blurted out the truth. "I came to Reno on business. I had no idea you would be at this hotel."

Immediately the window of vulnerability closed and the mask of worldliness she had seen earlier at the church slipped back into place. "I decided to stay here out of habit . . . or maybe even out of a touch of sentimentality," he said. "This is where my dad always booked a room when we came into town."

"And mine." She felt even more awkward in his presence than she had imagined she would. It took an instant for her to realize that it was because he was wearing an elegantly understated three-piece suit. Quickly she scanned her memory; she could remember seeing him in a suit only twice before. Both occasions had been funerals.

"Have you made plans for dinner?" he asked.

"No—yes!"

"Which is it?"

"No formal plans. I'll probably get something from room service."

He brushed the hair from his forehead. "My room . . . or yours?"

Danielle looked at him, confusion in her eyes. He was behaving as if the morning had never happened. And then the reason for his friendliness dawned on her. It made her sick to her stomach to realize he was trying to use a salesman's tactics on her. To him she was someone who needed to be sold on the idea that the casino he wanted to build was not as bad as she feared.

"I'm glad you took my warning seriously enough this morning to try to get me to change my mind, Steve. But don't bother. There isn't anything you could say to me, there aren't any charts you could show me that would make that aberration you want to build any more palatable."

"What in hell are you talking about?"

"Isn't that where people like you do most of their talking about business? Over a meal?"

"People like me?" His voice was deceptively calm. "Tell me about 'people like me,' Danny. Just how is it that we are different from folks like you?"

They were like two punch-drunk fighters who had heard the sound of the bell, and even knowing they would suffer further pain from the blows that would be struck, could not stay in their corners. "People like you see your beauty in asphalt and concrete. The only green you admire is money; the only smell, success."

"And people like you?"

"We see beauty in a quiet sunrise over a snow-capped mountain and have a penchant for breathing air that's free of exhaust fumes."

"And stagnate in your thoughts and opinions until your brains are as small and as narrow minded as your towns." Steve regretted the words the minute they had been spoken. He started to apologize, to suggest that they try to spend at least five minutes without arguing, but a wide grin curved Danny's mouth and all he could do was stare at her dumbfounded. He shook his head. "I don't understand."

"The insanity of what we are doing suddenly hit me. I was just thinking how incredible it is that we could once mean so much to each other, and then not see one another for ten years, and then when we *do* meet, the first thing we do is continue an argument that's a decade old."

He looked deeply into her eyes. "Danny, oh my beautiful Danny. The last thing in the world I want to do with you is fight."

And she knew she could have, if only for this night, all that she had dreamed. How desperately she wanted to say yes. But the price she would have to pay was too high—the trade too one-sided. Not even for the promise in his eyes could she give up her valley. She had to swallow back the pain before the words could be spoken. "Too much has come between us, Steve. We can't go back . . . there is no future."

"Then what's wrong with right now?"

"There's a casino standing between us."

His eyes narrowed ominously. "Don't try to blackmail me, Danny. As much as I want you, I won't bargain away the casino to get you. I have never believed in mixing business with pleasure. The result is rarely satisfactory in either area.

"How dare you?" Instantly tears of hurt and anger welled up in her eyes. Fiercely she wiped them away with the back of her hand. "If I were ever to sell myself, it would be for a hell of a lot more than a piece of land. And it would be to someone I wanted more than I want you."

Blindly she pushed her way past him and ran for the door. When she realized he had followed her outside she ducked into one of the casino's side entrances and then into the crowd at the dime slot machines.

In her rush to escape she bumped into a woman who was scooping dimes from the jackpot cavity at the base of one of the machines. The container was knocked to the floor, and dimes rolled in every direction. The woman glared at her, daring her to try to retrieve any of the coins.

"I'm terribly sorry," Danielle said, bending to help despite the woman's obvious reluctance to have her do so. Hurriedly dropping a fistful of dimes into the woman's outstretched hands she glanced over her shoulder and saw Steve coming her way. She shoved the last of the coins at the woman, mumbled another quick apology and frantically looked around for a new escape route. She spotted a discreet sign above a bank of blackjack tables directing the way to the women's lounge. With any luck she could merge into the crowd and then reach the lounge without being seen.

Making her way through the thickest gathering of people she bumped men whose hands immediately checked their wallets and women who clutched their purses tighter against their bodies, never glancing up to see who had touched them.

Danielle was struck by the grossness of the scene around her. A thick layer of stale smoke hung above the blinking lights of the clanging, ringing, grinding slot machines. Greedy, robotlike people fed a constant supply of dull silver-colored coins in the glassy-eyed hope that the machines would disgorge their elusive hoard and bring riches to the person who paid them homage, or at least a story to tell the folks back home. *And this was what Steve wanted to build in Star Valley.*

As Danielle stepped inside the elegantly formal lounge and leaned heavily against the cool marble wall she fought to bring her emotions under control. She felt like a wounded animal on the run. She hated herself for not having the courage or the strength to stand and fight.

Damn him. Damn him for so easily turning her into the confused indecisive young woman she had been ten years before. All she could think about, all she wanted to do, was to crawl back to the comfort of her home, to the land she loved, and forget all that had happened to her that day.

Knowing that Steve would not give up the search easily, she forced herself to remain in the lounge until she was sure he was gone. After that it was simply a matter of slipping from crowd to crowd until she was inside the valet-parking booth. Once there she waited for her truck to be brought to her.

Two hours later, she was home again.

4

THE LOUD KNOCK on the back door startled Danielle, making her drop the wide-tooth comb she had been using to untangle her freshly washed hair. A worried frown appeared as she grabbed her chenille bathrobe and hurried down the stairs, pulling the robe over her nightgown as she went. The lights had been out at both Ben's and Russell's houses when she had returned over an hour ago, and she knew that only trouble would bring them out of their beds in the middle of the night.

Opening the door she stepped back in surprise when she realized it was neither Ben nor Russ who had summoned her . . . it was Steve.

"May I come in?" he asked. He had changed from the suit he'd been wearing at the hotel to the jeans and western shirt he had worn that morning.

"If you are sincerely giving me a choice," she replied, "the answer is no."

He reached for her hand. "Then come out here. I don't care where we talk, as long as we do."

She pulled her hand out of his. "I'm tired and I have tons of work to do tomorrow that I should have done today. Besides, it seems to me that we've said too much to each other already."

"We've only said the wrong things—none of the right."

"Are there any?"

"Let me come in, Danny," he said softly.

She was so tired her fight was gone. She stepped aside and let him enter. Pulling the sash of her robe tighter, she nudged the door closed with her foot. "How did you know I had come back to the ranch?"

"I watched you leave and assumed this was where you would go."

So much for her cleverness and stealth. Not knowing what else to say, she asked, "Do you want something to eat? Drink?"

"No...." He paused. "Not unless the offer includes hot chocolate. I haven't had a decent cup since I left Nevada."

Despite her resolve not to, she smiled. "Why, I believe that's the saddest story I've heard in ever so long. Remind me before you leave town again and I'll give you the recipe."

"I'd rather have the cook."

Acting as if she hadn't heard him, Danielle opened the refrigerator. Still without replying she walked over to the stove and measured out two cups of the milk into a waiting pan. She was facing the stove when finally she said, "Why did you come here tonight, Steve?"

"To find out whether or not I was right about something."

"And were you?"

"Yes...."

She waited until it was obvious he had no intention of saying anything else. "Are you going to tell me what it was?"

"I'm not sure you would want to know."

"Is it about the casino? Is that why you've come?"

He walked over to stand beside her, leaning his hip against the counter and bending over to place his arm on the cool tiles that formed its low top. With an aching familiarity he casually reached up to brush a long strand of hair back over her shoulder and out of her way. "Would it be possible for us to set all of that aside tonight and pretend for a while that the casino doesn't exist? If only for a few hours, could we simply be two friends who haven't seen each other for a long time?"

"I don't know if that's—"

"Couldn't we at least try?"

No matter how she answered she would lose. To let him stay and to pretend they were merely friends would hurt as much in the long run as telling him he had to go now. "All right, Steve. We can pretend for a while—but we play the game by my rules." She focused all of her attention on stirring the chocolate milk as if it were a bomb that would go off at the slightest mistreatment. "You have to promise me that it won't go beyond *two old friends*. And...you have to promise me that you won't touch me again."

Steve stared at her a long time before answering. How could he promise something like that when he so desperately wanted to take her in his arms and hold her against him until the hurt of not being able to for so very, very long became a faded memory? "If that's truly what you want, I promise."

She seemed to perceptibly relax. Her obvious relief made him wonder what secret fears she harbored. "Would you at least tell me why you don't want me to touch you?"

She avoided looking at him as she reached for the cups and saucers. "Call it my concession to an otherwise ignored streak of self-preservation. I don't want to go through again what I went through the last time you left."

"You can't possibly believe that it was one-sided."

"And how would I know any differently?"

"Because you knew how much I loved you."

"I thought I did."

And then, as if a Rosetta stone had suddenly appeared to help him translate her words and emotions, he understood. She had waited for him to come back. She had never really believed him or fully comprehended when he had tried to make her understand that he would slowly die if he stayed at the ranch—that leaving was not one of two choices, but rather the only way he could survive. Not even her love had been able to chase away the ghosts of Frank and his father— ghosts that had haunted every waking hour he had spent in this valley. Nor could her love lessen the horror he had brought back with him from the war.

"You stayed here and waited for me to return, while I waited for the day you would love me enough to leave this valley and come to me. Even after years had passed I still held on to that dream," he said. "Until I found out you were married." His hand brushed through his hair. "I was given that particular piece of information the same day I opened the main offices of Eagle Enterprises in New York. My mother flew in from Nebraska for the big celebration and sort of casually, not knowing I'd care one way or the other, dropped the information that you were married. She honestly believed that you no longer mattered to me. I spent the next three days in a state of drunken self-pity."

A wistful half smile curved his mouth. "You see, I once had this crazy idea that if I were to work like hell and become very successful I could come back here and sweep you off your feet. You were supposed to be so impressed with what I had done that you would come back to New York with me. At least that's the way my daydream went."

Danielle struggled to take a breath, to expand her chest past a crushing heaviness. If he had come back to her carrying all of his possessions tied to the end of a stick she would have gone with him. "The marriage was a terrible mistake," she murmured. "I was so lonely at the time . . . my parents were so anxious for grandchildren. We were divorced six months after we were married. He was far too nice a person for me to let him continue to tie himself to someone who could never love him. I haven't seen or heard from him since."

She opened the cupboard beside her and mechanically added two plump marshmallows to each cup of chocolate. "I seem to have that effect on men."

"I didn't find out about your divorce until I came back to Nevada," he said. "I think my mother must have decided to do a little censoring after that one flagrant example of my unintelligent, off-the-wall behavior where you were concerned...or maybe she just never found out, herself. Mail is sometimes lost between here and Australia."

Danielle's eyes opened wide in surprise. "Australia?"

Steve's own eyes twinkled in amusement. "She married a sheep rancher she met on a South Sea cruise—sort of traded one kind of desert and one kind of ranch animal for another."

Danielle handed him his chocolate, passing so near that he could smell the still-damp freshness of her hair. His hand automatically went out to touch the softly shimmering mass where it lay against her back; he remembered times long ago when he had done the same thing as naturally as breathing.

She saw the movement from the corner of her eye and quickly stepped away from him, nearly spilling the foamy brown liquid she carried. Her reaction had been one of sheer panic. She used the anger that

flashed in her eyes to cover her growing need to have
him caress her, to touch her with loving hands. "You
promised," she breathed.

"I'm sorry," he said quietly. "I didn't think. I guess
I just wanted to see if your hair was as soft as I remembered." Their eyes had begun to communicate on
a level beyond their words. "Do you still save rain-
water to wash your hair in?"

She had stopped doing that a year after he had left,
only then realizing why she had gone to so much
bother in the first place. "No, my life became too filled
with important things to continue the habits of a
flighty girl."

"You were never flighty—perhaps a little young and
naive, but never flighty. And you were more of a
woman then than any woman I've met since."

"Don't say that, Steve. Don't say things that only
create dead-end roads." She turned and headed toward the arched doorway that led to the living room.

He followed her. When she reached to turn on a
lamp he stopped her, saying, "Leave it. I like the way
the moonlight fills the room. There's so much artifi-
cial light in New York at night that the effect of the
moon and stars aren't perceptible."

They sat opposite each other, Steve in a high-
backed wing chair, his legs propped up on the chair's
matching ottoman, Danielle on the sofa, her feet
curled up beneath her, her robe primly covering her
legs. After his eyes had adjusted to the room he could
see her as plainly as if the light had been turned on.

Slowly she drank her chocolate, unconsciously, sensuously licking the marshmallow from her lips before taking another sip. How many times had he pictured those lips pressed hungrily against his own? How many days, how many hours had they been apart? Even when he had held other women in his arms it had been Danny he had been making love to.

"Tell me about New York. Is it everything you dreamed it would be?" she asked.

"In some ways it's more, in some less. I was surprised when I first arrived and discovered that Manhattan was nothing like I had imagined it would be. For all of its glamour the city is like an ugly child and the people who live there are its doting defensive parents. Those who stay eventually come to tolerate and overlook the blemishes, because they grow to love the place with an insane, almost militant, passion."

"I can understand the feeling," she said. "I have had people look at me with total incomprehension when I try to tell them how I feel about Star Valley. They can't imagine anyone finding beauty in sagebrush and sand. They're usually the ones who ride through the area with their windows rolled up in air-conditioned cars and pronounce judgment without ever stepping outside." She took another sip of chocolate. "What did you do when you first left here?"

"Wandered for a while, looking for something I never found. Eventually I decided to go back to school. I scrimped by on odd jobs and the GI Bill. About halfway through my junior year I decided I wasn't learning anything I needed for what I wanted to do, so I quit and started investing in real estate. One thing led to another—Eagle Enterprises was the end result."

"Did you . . . were you. . . ."

"Ever married?"

She nodded, embarrassed that he had so easily known what she wanted to hear.

"The closest I ever came was someone I met a couple of years ago. Thankfully we had sense enough not to go through with it."

The logical question to follow would have been "Why?" She knew what an impassioned lover he could be and she could imagine how lonely he must have been. Why had he never asked someone to share his life with him? Her throat tightened. He *had* asked someone—ten years ago—and she had refused him.

Again there was silence between them. And then, "Are you happy, Danny?" A pause. "Do you ever wonder if you made the right choice?" When she didn't immediately answer, he softly added, "If you had it to do over, would you do everything the same?"

She shifted so that she could put her empty cup on the end table, stalling for time. "Sometimes I wonder how things would have been different if I had gone with you. I understand something now that I didn't then: my parents would have continued to run the ranch quite well without my being here. They would have gone on as they always had." The words were difficult for her to say; it was the first time she had given voice to thoughts that had formed slowly over a decade. "I'm sure that the pressure they put on me to try to take Frank's place was unconscious on their part. Had I accused them of doing so I sincerely believe they would not have understood how I felt.

"It wasn't until they died and the running of the ranch fell entirely to me that I finally admitted part of the reason I hadn't left with you was fear of the unknown. After all," she added defensively, as if trying to convince herself more than him, "I had lived here my entire life." She sighed. "But perhaps the main reason that I stayed behind when you begged me to go with you was the deep love I have for this valley."

His balloon of hope—that he might be able to change her mind and talk her into coming with him—suffered a brutal puncture, and as it deflated Steve felt a heaviness grow in his chest. "I've found out that doing something you love and doing it well are two of the most important things anyone ever has in life. I understand the double H has never been as prosperous as it's become since you took over."

"Then why does it bring me so little real happiness?" Her voice was a muted whisper. "Why are there times when I feel so empty?" She plucked at a tuft of chenille on her robe, blindly staring at her action through misty eyes and hoping Steve would not notice the tears that had formed.

"Danny...you still haven't answered me." He could scarcely breathe with the fear, the newfound hope that she would say what he so desperately wanted to hear. "Would you do any of it differently?"

"Then or now?" she hedged.

"Now."

What difference would it make how she answered? The problems that faced them would still be the same. To tell him that she loved him, that she always had, that she always would, would not put her ranch in New York nor bring his beloved New York any closer to Nevada. Nor would it make the casino he planned to build disappear. "I can't answer. . . ."

As if suddenly free of the restraints that had kept him from her, Steve left his chair and crossed the room. Sitting beside her, he took her hands in his, holding them tighter, closer, when she tried to pull away. "I won't accept that . . . I can't."

"Nothing has changed." She blinked, trying to keep the tears from spilling over her lashes. "Saying I would do things differently—that every day I hurt inside for the wasted years—isn't going to give them back to me."

"But what about now, Danny?" he insisted. "How would you answer me now if I were to ask you the same question I asked you ten years ago?"

A lone tear escaped to slide down her cheek. "If I could . . . I would say yes."

Almost afraid to speak for fear the moment would be lost, Steve softly asked, "What would stand in your way?"

She started to answer, but before she could speak he reached up to press his fingers against her lips. "No, not now. Tell me later." He could not chance hearing something that might destroy what was now between them. He could not close the door that had so magically swung open. "I love you, Danny," he whispered, moving his hand to let his fingers wipe the tear from her cheek. "I have always loved you. I will always love you." He heard her sharp intake of breath.

And then, as if the hidden bonds that had kept her from him had been broken, she collapsed into his arms. "Hold me, Steve." It was as if the words had been wrenched from her soul. "Make me forget that there ever was a yesterday. Don't let me think about tomorrow."

His hand tangled in her hair as he drew her closer to him. Inhaling the heady aroma that was Danielle he held his breath in his lungs. His cheek and then his lips pressed softly against the top of her head in a lingering caress.

Being in his arms again felt so right, as if they had never been apart. Her heart, her soul, were home. When thoughts of tomorrow tried to intrude Danielle pushed them aside. This night was here, a gift to cherish forever on the lonely evenings that would necessarily follow.

Her hands went to his face and she held him away from her so that she could look into his eyes. "I wish I knew the words—how can I make you understand how much I love you?"

"We've wasted so much time," he said.

"We have tonight . . . let's not spoil it with regrets."

"I want more than tonight, Danny. I want—"

"Please, don't. . . ." Her eyes begged him to stop before their differences were again separating them.

"Tonight is not enough," he said. "I refuse to accept that you believe it is." He pulled her to him. His kiss was filled with such yearning she knew he would never let it be just tonight between them. With that kiss he made love to her, coaxing, leading, thrusting, giving her a message that told of his need for her to be with him forever. Suddenly she stopped caring about rules or problems or consequences.

She wanted him. Her body cried out its need for him. Feelings she thought she had smothered were rekindled and now reached out from the hidden corners of her being. The strength of those feelings stunned her. She could feel her control leaving like water from a cupped hand.

She wanted to lead, to show him that she, too, needed him, but she could only follow as he took her deeper into the mindlessness of out-of-control passion. With a deft gracefulness he put his hands under her arms and lifted her, swinging her to him so that she sat on his lap. He pressed his face to her breast, exhaling into the chenille as he nuzzled the rounded flesh. His warm moist breath sent a scorching message through the fabric. With a gasp Danielle arched her back, silently asking him, in a language as ancient as man, to possess her.

His hands went around her waist. He held on to her as if he were afraid she would suddenly disappear. This dream had been his so often. And so often he had awakened to the hard reality of a morning without her. Tonight was not enough. If he were to have her tonight and not have her tomorrow, it would destroy him. There had to be a way they could work things out between them.

But his fears and thoughts were again swept away by a wave of mindless passion as Danielle's soft moan pulled him deeper and deeper into a world where only that moment counted. Never had he known such raw need. Never had he felt so little control.

In a murmured half sentence he asked her if she wanted to go upstairs; a breathless " . . . upstairs is so far away. . ." was her answer. When he opened her robe to kiss her breasts through the thin cotton nightgown, she gasped her hunger, her need to feel his mouth against her bare flesh. She left his lap and stood in front of him, letting the robe fall to the floor. Silhouetted against the bright moonlight streaming through the window, her naked body clearly outlined under the thin cotton, she seemed a mystical temptress.

Steve reached for the lace-trimmed hem of her gown where it brushed against her ankles. As he lifted the material, he let the backs of his hands brush against the length of her sculptured thighs in a continuous urgent caress. When he stood and pulled the gown over her head, she lowered her arms to his waist.

Dipping her fingers beneath his belted jeans, she tugged at his shirt until it was free. Standing on tiptoe, she put her arms around his neck and then purposely, erotically let her breasts make contact with his chest. His hands went to her sides and then her back, pressing her closer, melding her roundness to his planes, coaxing and then demanding that she feel the depth of his need for her.

A muted cry of reciprocal need vibrated in her throat as their mouths met in an explosive kiss. Steve's hands coursed the arch of her back in enraptured strokes, then moved on to cup the firm flesh of her buttocks and draw her closer to him still.

Breaking the kiss, he buried his face in the full sweeping waves of her hair. "I need you, Danny," he said, his voice filled with a depth of longing that reached past her reasoning to touch her soul. With his words, with his actions, he had told her that the years, the months, the days, the hours they had been apart had been the same journey through hell for him that they had been for her.

"As I need you . . ." she answered. Her hands again went to his waist. When she had trouble opening the unusual clasp of his belt, he helped her. When she purposely fumbled opening the button on his jeans, he softly groaned his pleasure. Soon the last of his clothing joined the other pieces that lay around them.

For a golden moment they looked at each other, and their eyes communicated their love, their need for each other, more profoundly than any words they might have spoken. Finally Steve reached for her in the special timeless way of lovers and she eagerly came to him. Her body, her heart, her very soul gave what her mind could not.

Gently Steve lowered Danielle onto the couch. He then eased himself between her parted thighs and entered her. She cried her welcome. He caught the cry and held it to him as his mouth closed over hers. They moved together in an ancient rhythm, seeking, giving pleasures that had been too long denied. Soon, too soon, they were on a one-way journey. . . .

DANIELLE WAS LYING on the couch in the loving warmth of Steve's arms when the full impact of what they had done hit her. She closed her eyes in a weary sigh, untangled herself from him and reached for her robe. She dressed with her back to him as if somehow ashamed of what had passed between them.

As clearly as if he could read her thoughts, Steve understood her actions. He reached for her hand, bringing the work-roughened palm to his mouth. "Danny," he murmured, "listen to me."

"Not now, Steve," she said, still not looking at him.

"We have to talk."

"Not now." There was a note of desperation in her voice. She pulled her hand from his and walked to the window, where she tried to tie the sash of her robe with fingers that trembled. Oh, dear, sweet merciful God, her mind cried, how was she ever going to get

through the days and nights that were ahead of her now?

She heard the sounds of Steve dressing behind her. When his footsteps headed in her direction she said, "I think you should leave now, Steve." The footsteps ceased. "And I don't think it would be a good idea for us to see each other again." She felt his hands on her shoulders firmly turning her so that she had to face him.

"I'm going to pretend I didn't hear that." His voice was filled with anger. "I told you before, Danny, that tonight was not enough. I meant it. I'm not going to fade dramatically away like one of your damned Nevada sunsets just because I don't fit into your scheme of things."

"Why won't you acknowledge that what stands between us is more than the simplistic picture you insist on painting? You seem to think that if we simply ignore our differences, they'll conveniently go away."

"It's a hell of a lot easier than trying to ignore what my life is like without you."

"Don't you dare try to make me the heavy in this—"

"Because I have the audacity to tell you how much you mean to me? How lonely I am without you?" He took his hands from her shoulders and shoved them into his pockets. When he spoke again his voice was deceptively calm. "As I recall, this argument led us exactly nowhere ten years ago. I can't see any sense in taking it up again now. I have some things that I have to clear up in Reno. I'll be back when I've finished. You know why I'm going and you know why I'll be back. I'll want an answer when we see each other again, Danny."

"You're as pigheaded and as self-centered as you always were." She turned away from him. "It's still me who's expected to sacrifice. Nothing has changed. You want me to give up everything to follow you. Do you honestly think that after ten years you can breeze in here and expect me to abandon everything I've worked so hard for to become Mrs. Stephen Zackery Maddox?"

"Do you love me?" he asked quietly, the anger suddenly gone, a look of naked vulnerability in its place.

"Damn you!" she breathed.

"Are you going to deny us out of some inherent streak of stubbornness the lifetime of happiness we can bring each other, just because one of us has to sacrifice something and in this case it's you?" His voice grew softer yet pleading. "I'll make it up to you, Danny. I know what I'm asking. I know what our life would be like together."

He stared down at her. "I also know what our life is like without each other. We've shared so much tragedy—don't you think it's about time we shared some joy?" When she still didn't answer, he sighed heavily and went on. "Weigh it all. Put it all on a balance scale and see how being together measures up to being alone. I'll be back in a couple of days for your answer."

He bent over, placed a kiss on the top of her head, turned and was gone.

5

THE NIGHT PROVED to be impossibly long, each minute seeming an hour as Danielle tossed in her bed, vacillating between rage and frustration. Instead of bringing release from the ache that burned deep in her loins, making love with Steve had only made her more sharply aware of her day-to-day loneliness. She knew that, because the memory had been reinforced, her overpowering longing would not quickly or easily retreat to the subconscious where she had kept it under a margin of control for so many years.

Again she glanced at the clock. Still an hour to go before daybreak. With a sigh of disgust she threw back the covers and climbed out of bed. If she went to sleep now she would feel drugged all day.

She was in the kitchen frying bacon when she heard a soft tapping on the back door. Before she could stop it a quick stab of hope made her think it might be Steve returning. Angry at her reaction, she purposely took her time going to the door.

"Hi, Missy," Ben said, ignoring her scowl. "Got enough for two?"

She forced a smile, determined not to make Ben the recipient of her bad mood. "There's always enough for you. Come on in."

"I saw the car was gone so I figured it was okay if I came over."

"What car?"

A slow smile bunched his mustache under his nose. "Aw, come on, Danny. You wouldn't want to keep something like this all to yourself, would you?"

"How did you know?"

"You must've been taking a shower when he got here last night or were just being contrary, 'cause nobody answered here at the house when he first came. So Steve just moseyed down to my place for a little visit." His eyes twinkled mischievously. "He sure looks good. That city life seems to agree with him."

"What did he tell you?"

"About?"

"Don't beat around the bush. What did he say he was doing here?"

Ben walked over to the stove and poured himself a cup of coffee. "Said he came back to see if you were still as stubborn as you used to be."

Danielle put the bacon on a paper towel to drain, started the toast and added another four eggs to the bowl, forcefully whipping them into a froth before pouring them into the frying pan. "Why am I the one who's stubborn when he is every bit as adamant and unbending about where we should live?"

After adding a dollop of milk to his coffee, Ben closed the refrigerator and moved to sit at the table. "I don't know how things are between you two now, but last time you were faced with the same choice, I think you should've gone with him."

"Why?" She swung around to face him. "Because that's what women have always done?"

"You could've adapted back then, might even have come to like city life. But Steve wouldn't be half the man he is today if he'd've stayed here. He was hurting real bad when he left. I've seen that look before. I don't believe he had any real choice—" he sipped his coffee "—but you did."

"That's not fair. My feelings were every bit as strong as Steve's. Frank's death put as much pressure on me as it did on him."

"Only I don't think you realized just what Steve was going through then. I believe you half expected he would come back after he got some of the wandering out of his system."

She took their plates to the table. The fire was gone from her voice. "It was all I had. Was it so wrong to hope?"

"It wasn't hope that motivated what you did, Danny. You took a gamble that he couldn't stay away and you lost." When she started to turn away he reached for her hand. "I've never seen someone pay such a terrible price for a lost wager in all my life."

She left her hand in his. "I suppose that means that you think I should go with him now?"

With his other hand he lifted a slice of bacon to his mouth, took a bite and thoughtfully chewed. "I can't answer that one. It's been a long time . . . people change. All I can tell you is that when you get a little older you begin to realize how important it is to have someone you care about share the little things of life— like a sunset or a memory. Stubbornness and who was right or wrong don't seem to matter so much."

He was telling her things she didn't want to hear. "Are you going to wax poetic on me, Ben?"

"It won't work, Danny. You're not going to get me to change the subject 'til I've said all I'm going to say."

Leaning back in her chair she held her coffee cup against her cheek and stared at him. "Then spit it out. We've got a lot of work to get done today."

"I don't want to see that casino built any more than you do. . . ."

"But?"

"This land is going to be here long after we're both gone, and trying to keep everyone else out is only going to last as long as we're around to fight. What harm is it going to do if we just let them in fifty years or so early?"

"I can't believe you said that."

"Neither can I. But if it means you could live those fifty years with a man you love, the trade-off would be more than worth it. You're not getting any younger, you know. If you don't start out on having some kids pretty soon, you're gonna wake up some morning and it's gonna be too late."

Danielle groaned. "Thanks, Ben. That's all I needed to hear."

"It's a fact of life, Missy. And if you don't have any kids, who's going to take over this place when you're gone?"

"That was a low blow." She took a sip of coffee and absently pushed her half-eaten food aside. "Besides, what makes you think city-raised kids would even want to inherit a few thousand acres of sagebrush and sand?"

He met her gaze, smiling conspiratorially. "You'd see to that."

"You make it sound so easy."

"How easy would it be to spend the *next* ten years alone?" he asked softly.

Footsteps on the porch drew their attention to the back door. At the tentative knock Danielle called out, "Come in, Sean."

An eight-year-old boy with bright red hair and doelike brown eyes opened the door and stuck his head inside. "Morning, Miz Hartman, Mr. Ben. Papa said to tell you he's ready to leave as soon as y'all are."

"Tell him we'll be right there." Danielle smiled at the departing boy and the loud thumping sounds he made as he took the stairs two at a time. "He looks more like his dad every day."

"Yeah, Russ is real proud of him. And of Erica, too. She's gonna be a real looker someday—just like her momma." He stared at her meaningfully. "It'd be a shame if you never got to have one of your own to watch grow up and take pride in."

Danielle's eyes narrowed. "Are you through?"

"Pretty much."

"Good. Then why don't you clean up the dishes while I finish getting dressed?"

THOUGHTS OF ALL that had happened in the past twenty-four hours mixed with Ben's words and followed Danielle throughout the day, distracting her so badly that she almost hit one of the wranglers when she backed the cattle truck out of a field.

"Hey, Miss Hartman," the ranch hand called. "Didn't anyone ever tell you that good help is hard to get! You should be a little more careful with us workers."

She laughed appreciatively at his good humor over what could have been a terrible accident. "I promise I'll remember. Next time I'll aim for Randy."

He grinned and waved goodbye as he and Russ took off toward town. She was still watching his truck disappear in a cloud of dust when Ben walked up to stand beside her. Putting his arm around her shoulders and pulling her close, he said, "Think maybe you could take the rest of the day off?"

"Is the crew threatening to mutiny?"

"Only one or two. The rest are under control."

She continued to stare at the lengthening ribbon of dust. "I wish I could say that I can't understand what's happening to me." Shoving her hands into her pockets, she sighed heavily. "I don't know what I would do with myself if I took the afternoon off."

"You could go into Reno and do some shopping."

Danielle turned to stare at him as if she feared for his sanity. "Shopping? Why would I want to go shopping?"

"Just thought you might like to get something pretty for when Steve comes back."

A slow smile curved her mouth. "Believe me, Ben," she said, her voice low and husky, "it isn't the wrapping that Steve's interested in seeing." And for the first time in her memory, she could have sworn she saw Ben Reed blush.

It took Danielle two agonizing days to reach a decision. On the morning of the third day, just as she was getting out of bed, she heard the sound of a car coming up the long driveway to the ranch. Sensing that it was Steve, she dashed to the bathroom to splash water on her face, brush her teeth and grab her robe. She was frantically running a brush through her sleep-tossed hair when she heard his footsteps on the porch and abandoned the attempt. Her feet barely touched the runners as she flew down the stairs to greet him, flinging the door open as he was preparing to knock.

Carrying a huge, wilted bouquet of haphazardly mixed flowers he greeted her. "I've come courting, Miss Hartman," he said formally.

"Why, Mr. Maddox. What a surprise. Won't you please come in?" She made a grand sweeping gesture.

Pointedly looking at the flowers, she coyly added, "By any chance are those for me?"

"As a matter of fact, they are. When I offered them to Ben, he said they weren't his favorites, so he suggested I bring them up to you."

Her eyes widened. "You stopped in to see Ben before you came here?"

He smiled. "If I had known what kind of reaction it would bring I might have done just that. But to answer you, no, I came straight here. Nothing could keep me away from you one minute longer this particular morning." She noticed that as he handed her the sad-looking flowers, his hand trembled.

"Thank you," she said softly as she went over to the sink and opened an overhead cupboard to take out a tall cut-glass vase. Waiting for the water to fill the vase, she glanced out the window at the false sunrise and wondered what time her day would start in New York. Then she almost dropped the flowers and whirled around to stare at Steve. "What time did you leave Reno this morning?"

He shrugged noncommittally.

"You can't possibly not know," she said. "You must have left in the middle of the night."

"Actually it was a few hours before. I had planned to wait around the hotel until this morning...." He shrugged again. "Obviously I didn't."

"I don't understand. Where did you go? Where have you been all this time?"

"Down the road."

"What road?"

"The ranch road."

"All night?"

"The better part of it."

"Why?"

"Just before I cut off the main highway, I remembered what a grump you can be when you don't get enough sleep. My staying the night in the car was totally self-serving. I wanted you to be in the best possible mood when we talked."

As the impact of what he had done hit her she slowly turned back to the sink and mindlessly tried to prop the wilted head of a rose up against the stem of a drooping daisy. "For future reference," she said, "you might like to know I outgrew that particular idiosyncrasy quite a while ago. Besides, you could have come anytime last night and found me already awake."

"I wish I had known. . . ."

An awkward silence grew between them. Steve cleared his throat. *Now,* he told himself. *Now was* the moment to ask. The delay was torture. "Uh . . . I noticed when I drove by this morning that your lower field looked pretty bad."

She set the flowers aside and turned to face him again. "We've been having a lot of trouble with the sprinklers." She wiped her wet hands on her robe. "They're fine as long as we stand and watch over them, but the minute we leave, they jam." Nervously she twisted a lock of hair around her finger. "With everything else that's going on I can't afford to leave a man there all day just to watch them and wait for something to go wrong. So until the new parts come in, it's catch as catch can." Her hair had become hopelessly knotted.

"We'll just have to supplement our own crop a little more than usual this winter," she went on. "I've checked with Harley Meyers and he said that he should be able to supply me with whatever I need." She crossed her arms over her breasts and leaned against the counter. "Ben's tried for the last two years to get me to put in another field but—" Unable any longer to ignore the haunted look in Steve's dark brown eyes, Danielle abruptly stopped. "You didn't come all the way out here to talk about the trouble I'm having with my hay and sprinklers."

His hands resting lightly on his hips, Steve stared down at the shiny linoleum. "You're right." When he again looked at her, his face was full of misery.

"Dammit, Danny. I feel like a kid going after his first date. What's the matter with me?" His hands slipped into his front pockets. "I came back to Nevada with such arrogant confidence. I haven't suffered a defeat in anything I've tried since I left. And yet here I am, a tongue-tied adolescent terrified of a wisp of a woman. I can't believe how hard this is for me. Every part of me is screaming to get it over with, but somewhere inside my head a little voice keeps telling me that as long as I don't, there's still hope." He sought a clue to her feelings in her eyes, and when he couldn't find the reassurance he needed he took a deep shaky breath.

"I wish I knew a way to say this that would make you understand what your answer means to me...but I don't." He reached up to touch her cheek, his hand openly trembling. In a voice little more than a husky whisper he said, "Danielle Annamarie Hartman, will you marry me?"

She took his hand in hers and raised the palm to her lips. "Yes," she murmured softly against the smooth skin.

"Yes?" he breathed.

She nodded.

"Yes, you'll marry me and come to New York with me?"

Again she nodded.

A pent-up sigh of relief escaped his lips as he pulled her into his arms and held her tightly against him. "When did you decide? Why didn't you call me to let me know?"

"I only decided yesterday. I didn't try to contact you because I needed time to get used to the idea. I'm still not sure it's the right decision. I only know that it seemed as if there wasn't really any other one for me to make. I don't want to spend the next ten years the way I did the last ten." She could feel his heart beating heavily in his chest.

"I will do everything in my power to make you happy," he vowed. "I love you. My God, Danny, how I love you."

She tilted back her head and welcomed the loving warmth of his kiss. "When?" she asked as his mouth brushed softly against her temple.

"This afternoon?"

"You're kidding." And when he didn't answer, "Aren't you?"

"If you want to be married here in Nevada, it's either today or not for a week."

"But I can't be ready to leave in a month, let alone a week. There are a hundred things that still have to be done before I can even consider leaving. We've only begun to vaccinate the cattle. And the sprinklers—"

"Danny, there are always a hundred things to do on a ranch. You'll never leave if you wait for them all to be finished."

"But—"

"Have you talked to Ben about this?"

"Not yet."

"Why don't I go down—"

A note of panic marked her next words. "I don't understand. Why does it have to be today or a week from today? Why not after? Why not in between?"

"Because I have to fly home this afternoon. There are meetings this next week I have to attend, meetings my secretary was unable to change. After they're over we'll have the following week all to ourselves."

She stared at the silver-rimmed snaps on his shirt, fighting the growing sense of panic that she was being maneuvered into a corner. "Do you know I have no real idea what you do for a living? I know nothing about what you do every day—what you like, what you dislike."

"Stop it, Danny. We know all we need to know about each other."

"I can't. This afternoon is . . . it's too soon. Please understand, Steve. To just get up and leave this place, to leave Ben like that . . . I simply can't do it. I have to at least say goodbye."

He held her face between his hands and looked deeply into her eyes. "I'm fighting my own fears, Danny. A perverse voice keeps whispering in my ear that if I don't insist you come with me right now you'll change your mind and never come." He pulled her to him and rested his chin gently on the top of her head. "It will be hard to be away from you. Every day will be hell for me. Even after waiting all this time, a mere week longer seems an eternity."

"I'm not going to change my mind, Steve." She released the breath she had been holding. "And deep inside of me I know you're right about the ranch—there will never be a good time to leave. The only way I'll ever let go of this place is to just walk away from it. But give me that week. Ben and I will work things out while you're gone." Pressing her forehead against the smooth cotton of his shirt she added, "Ben shouldn't have any trouble running the place without me—he could manage what I do blindfolded, sitting backward on a three-legged horse."

"We both know you're lying," he murmured against her hair. "But if believing that nonsense makes leaving any easier, I won't argue the point."

"There's one more thing we have to finish." He took his arm from around her waist to pull a folded document out of his back pocket. "This is what's kept me away from you these past three days. It might change things a little for Ben, depending on how you decide to handle it."

She took the papers and walked to the table to sit down.

"Before you look at what I've given you, Danny, I want you to know something. I would have done this no matter what your answer was today."

A puzzled frown on her face, Danny slowly opened the official-looking document. It took several seconds for her to realize what Steve had done. "Why?" she asked softly as she stared at his bold signature across the bottom of a deed transferring all interest in the Maddox ranch to Danielle Annamarie Hartman.

"The instant I realized the casino had nothing to do with my coming back here, it stopped being important." He came over to sit down beside her. "There's a part of me I've been trying to deny for a long time— a part that will always be tied to this place. I know now that the casino idea was merely a subconscious yearning to return. I had to find out, once and for all, if there was any chance for us." His hand brushed back the hair that had fallen across his forehead. "I don't want to see a casino complex on that land any more than you do—it just took me a little longer to admit what an atrocity it would have been. So now it's in your safekeeping, with no strings attached. The land and everything on it is in your name; it will be yours for as long as you want it, to do with what you will."

"You were going to give to me even if I said no to you today?"

A wonderful smile lit his eyes. "That was the idea— but I don't think I could ever have accepted no for an answer. You said you had no idea what I do for a living. Well, basically I take companies that are supposedly impossible to turn around and I make them profitable again. Surely you don't think I would have given up where you were concerned?"

She gave him her best "just who do you think you're trying to fool, fella," look. "Then why did I see such uncertainty in your eyes when you came here this morning?"

The playfulness, the bravado, disappeared. "I've never played for such high stakes."

"I love you, Steve. Being with you is more important than anything else in my life." She carefully folded the legal document in front of her. "I suppose you realize, though, that doubling the size of the ranch presents even more problems about being able to leave in a week's time."

He took the papers from her and tossed them onto the counter. Pulling her into his arms, he held her so that their hips rested against each other's. "Nothing presents that big a problem." As he kissed her eagerly responsive lips a deep wave of swelling desire washed over him. "I'm so afraid I'm going to wake up tomorrow and all of this is going to fade away."

She wrapped her arms around his neck. "Kiss me again," she demanded. When he acquiesced and brought his mouth to hers she pulled back before letting the kiss deepen. Caressing his lips with her tongue she purposely yet timidly sought entry, as if delving into the sweetness for the first time. With each tentative stroke she grew a little bolder, went a little farther until at last she explored the satiny interior. He welcomed her and with an eloquent moan urged her to be bolder still.

She broke the kiss and huskily whispered, "Do you still think I'm just a dream?"

"Only if my dreaming has become immensely improved."

She started to answer but her words were lost against his seeking mouth.

Their world shrank around them until it consisted of a mist of fine explosive particles composed of the growing need they had for each other. A few minutes before, in response to an inbred sense of modesty, Danielle might have protested that they should delay their lovemaking, that she was expected by the others to begin the day's work. Now she only knew how desperately she wanted Steve to finish the act of love they had begun—to bring some satiation to the ache that now gripped her to the exclusion of common sense.

Steve brushed moist kisses against her lavender-scented skin. Leaving a tingling trail from her mouth to her ear, he murmured, "I don't know...what to do with you...my dearest, darling Danny."

She shifted her weight, pressing her hips invitingly against his as a mischievous smile lit her eyes. "You couldn't possibly have forgotten. It's only been a couple of days."

A low chuckle preceded his next words. "Not likely." And as if to prove his point his hands traveled from the curve of her waist to the sides of her breasts, where he softly pressed his palms against the flesh that ached for his bold touch. When, with his thumbs, he began to make slow concentric circles over the thickness of her robe, she could feel her nipples tighten and grow hard in response. His hands went back to her sides to pull her closer to him, then slipped beneath the silkiness of her hair to make unhurried caressing movements against her back, her waist, her hips.

Warm and teasing, his breath invaded the inside of her ear. "Come to New York with me. There's nothing that has to be done that can't wait," he pleaded. "I will never last the week without you."

"I can't...leave yet," she protested. "Stay with me."

His hands returned to her waist, moving upward until they brushed the exquisitely sensitive undersides of her breasts in tender loving strokes. "If only I could."

Purposefully she began to unsnap the closures of his shirt, each soft sound an erotic announcement of her intent. When the last of the snaps had been opened she slowly moved the plaid material aside with inquisitive questing kisses. An incredible wash of memories overcame her as she tasted again the slight saltiness of his skin and inhaled the spicy fragrance of his soap. How well she had known these things—how poignant a part of her past they were.

As she crossed the hard muscled plain of his chest to gently, possessively take a nipple between her teeth, she heard his quick intake of breath. A sound, partially her name, partially an indistinguishable groan of pleasure, rode on the exhaled air.

She felt his fingers seek her sash, and she moved her hips to allow him access. When his hand slipped inside her robe and down the smooth cotton of her gown to press warmly against the flat of her stomach, she raised up on tiptoe, urging him to be bolder.

Steve read her signs of arousal and knew she wanted him with an urgency that matched his own. Bending over, he swept her into his arms. "Are you sure you want this to happen now?" he asked, knowing she would at the very least have to face inquisitive looks when she appeared in front of the ranch hands later.

"I'll manage," she said softly, burying her face in his shoulder.

"They'll see the car."

"They've *seen* the car. My reputation was probably ruined forever three nights ago. Nothing is secret or sacred around here." She looked up and grinned at him. "If I have the name, I'm darned well going to play the game."

Just then a loud thumping sounded on the back porch.

"Oh, no," Danielle gasped. "It's Sean! Quick, put me down."

Her feet met the floor at the same time Sean's knuckles met the doorframe. "Just a minute," she called out hastily, frantically trying to adjust her robe. But to someone who for more than three years had never heard any answer besides "Come in," his reaction was automatic and instant.

"Morning, Miss Hart—' His mouth dropped open in surprise when he saw Steve standing in the middle of the room trying to shove Danielle behind him. His eyes darted from one to the other before he snapped his head back behind the door like a terrified turtle and thumped down the stairs.

"Who was that?" Steve asked.

"Russ Edwards's boy," she sighed. When she saw that he still didn't understand she added, "Russ is the top hand I hired about four years ago. More than likely he will be the one to take Ben's place when I leave and Ben takes my place."

Steve pulled her back into his arms, giving her a quick kiss on the tip of her nose. "Should I go after him and explain my presence?"

Holding on to the sides of his shirt and tilting her head up for a more accurate kiss, she snuggled closer. "Someone will tell him who you are. It seems to me

that we had other plans." When she saw the concerned frown she added, "Don't worry. It'll be all
right. We may live in different houses around here but
we're like one big family. Sean will find his dad and
tell him what he saw and Russ will explain everything."

"If you recall, Ben is the only person around here
who knows who I am."

As if to add a blood-chilling emphasis to his words,
a loud commotion drew their attention to the back
door. Before Danielle could move to see what was
going on, the door burst open. Russ stood on the
threshold, a shotgun in his hands. "Are you okay, Miss
Hartman?" he asked, his voice low and threatening.

Steve knew better than to move or to try to explain
what was going on. He recognized the protective wary
gleam in Russ's eyes. He was expressing a fear that
most isolated ranchers had in common—that they
would someday be the victim of a criminal who figured them easy prey. For years people in the region
had been known to subscribe occasionally to the an-
tiquated rule that had once governed the area—shoot
first, ask questions later.

Danielle pulled her robe tighter. "I'm fine, Russ."
A smile twitched at the corners of her mouth. So much
for a quiet little interlude. "Oh, and by the way, I'd like
you to meet Steve Maddox. A long time ago he lived
next door." Turning to Steve, she added, "Steve, this
is Russ Edwards."

Before walking into the room to take Steve's hand Russ broke the gun barrel and pulled out two shells. "I'm pleased to meet you, Mr. Maddox. I've heard quite a bit about you from Ben. Sorry I didn't think long enough to put two and two together."

"I understand," Steve said. "I'm afraid it should be me who's apologizing. I certainly didn't mean to scare your boy like that." A mop of red curls appeared around the door.

"No problem. He'll be fine once he gets over being embarrassed."

Before anything else could be said Ben came walking up the stairs. "What's all the commotion?" he asked, striding into the kitchen.

Danielle sighed and shook her head in feigned disgust. She stopped trying to hold her bathrobe closed with her hands and reached for the sash, no longer fooling herself that she might be able to pretend that she and Steve had been preparing to share a cup of coffee and not a glorious morning of lovemaking. "Well, now that the gang's all here," she said, "I guess it's as good a time as any to make my announcement."

Sean's voice broke in from somewhere on the porch. "You getting married, Miz Hartman?"

From behind her she heard Steve chuckle. "Yes, Sean. I'm getting married," she answered.

Ben let out a whoop as he stepped forward, pulled her into his arms and hugged her in a breath-catching embrace. So that only she could hear he said softly,

"Congratulations, Missy. I knew you had the guts to do it. I'm as proud of you as I can be."

She ran her fingers across his freshly shaven cheek as she looked deeply into his ageless eyes. In a voice as soft she replied, "That doesn't mean I'm not scared, Ben."

"I know you are. That just makes me prouder." He kissed her forehead, hung one arm over her shoulder and thrust his other hand at Steve. "All my best, Steve. You two know what hell is like; it's about time you had a taste of heaven."

Steve took Ben's hand, feeling the love and good wishes the older man extended as surely as he felt the callused flesh. There was so much he could say, so much he wanted to say. He knew that Danny would never have been able to come to a decision as freely as she had if Ben hadn't been in the background encouraging her, ready to take over and run the ranch should she ask. In the end it was a simple, heartfelt "Thank you, Ben," that sufficed.

"Miss Hartman," Russ chimed in. "I want you to know that I'm real pleased for you. And you too, Mr. Maddox." He reached for Steve's hand.

When the well wishes had been said and acknowledged a silence settled, until finally Russ stepped back and cleared his throat. "I think I'd better get everyone rounded up and working or we'll be branding and vaccinating clear into next winter."

Ben nodded in agreement. "Go ahead and get started without me," he said. "I'll join you quick as I can."

When Russ and Sean were gone Ben turned to Danielle. "I could be wrong but I don't think he's real crazy about what's going on."

"He'll come around once he realizes that nothing is going to change around here," she said.

"Now how do you figure that?" Ben interjected, a thread of anger in his tone. "Oh, we'll get along all right without you running the place," he went on, not waiting for her answer. "Ranches have been around for a long time. There isn't anything so special about running them that someone else can't step in and take over if they have a lick of sense about them. But don't you go saying that you won't be missed, 'cause dammit, Danny, if the truth be told, you're going to take the lifeblood right out of the place when you go."

She was too stunned to answer him.

"Now I'm only going to say one more thing about all this, then I want to leave it behind and get on with the business at hand," he went on. "I love you like you was my own. I want you to be happy. I want it so bad that I'm letting you go without so much as an argument to try to get you to stay, even though I know I'm going to be one hell of a lonely old man without you around to keep me company."

Her throat ached with the effort to keep tears from filling her eyes. "Be happy for me, Ben," she managed to say.

"Ah, Danny." He hugged her close. "It's only an ornery streak of selfishness that keeps me from jumping with joy to see that sparkle back in your eyes. It's been gone such a long time."

"New York's not that far...."

"That's right. And don't you forget it." He kissed her soundly on the mouth. "I've got work to do," he said gruffly. Nodding to Steve, he picked up his hat and left.

Danielle stared at the door. "He's never kissed me like that before," she said softly.

Steve came up to stand beside her, resting his hands on her shoulders. "He's going to miss you." He pulled her to him so that her back rested against his chest. "This week is going to be hard to get through, Danny...."

"Even harder than I had imagined, it seems."

"I—"

"I'm not going to change my mind, Steve. Don't go to New York worrying that I might be unwilling to leave here when you return because I won't. I love you and I want a life with you more than I want anything else. I'm not stepping into this blindly; I know it's going to be hard for me to adapt to a completely different life-style. Last night when I couldn't get to sleep, I lay there and tried to imagine what it would be like to live in a big city." She laughed lightly. "Reno was the only big city I could imagine."

A chill tiptoed down Steve's spine. She sounded so earnest and determined, so positive that she could transfer her life simply because she wanted to so very badly. Should he tell her that Reno and New York had about as much in common as the Nevada desert had with the North Pole? No, better to let her discover that for herself. If he told her she would never understand. Not yet. Her point of reference, the life she had lived up until now, was a 180-degree-turn from the world she would soon occupy.

How could he describe the view from the World Trade Towers or relay the magic of a buggy ride through Central Park in the spring, when neither could be compared to anything she had ever known? There was so much he wanted her to see, to share—a hot pretzel from a street vendor, an opening night at the Metropolitan Opera House, cappuccino at a sidewalk café on a warm summer evening. "I'll be back here to get you as soon as I can, Danny. Wait for me." It was an unspoken plea more than a request.

She snuggled against him. "After what we've been through a week should seem like a blink of an eye, but somehow it doesn't. It seems like forever." The thought caused a heavy silence between them. Forcefully Danielle tried to lighten the mood. "Are we going to go on a honeymoon?"

"We can go any place you would like to go."

She thought for a moment. "I'd like to see the ocean. I never have."

He smiled, knowing what special joy it was going to bring him to show her the things she had never before seen. "Hawaii?" he suggested.

No, it was not Hawaii she wanted to see. Hawaii was not the secret place she had promised herself she would visit one day. "Would you mind if we saved Hawaii for another time?" She didn't wait for his answer. "I know this is going to sound crazy, but I would love to see Monterey, California."

"Monterey it is," he answered easily. "I'll make the arrangements." His breath was warm in her hair. "I assume you're going to tell me why you chose Monterey?"

"John Steinbeck... I've always wanted to see the places he wrote about. They seemed so different from here, yet strangely the same."

"You'll have to tell me about them." He nuzzled her ear, gently invading the sensitive outer circle. "If you recall, Mrs. Grady threw me out of Senior English. It was before we got to Steinbeck. I didn't get back in again until they were in the middle of studying writers from the South."

"I do remember. You and Frank put quick-drying glue on her chair and they had to cut her skirt off to get her free."

He laughed softly. "That was another time; she never did prove we were involved in the chair episode. The stunt that finally got us thrown out was dismantling her Volkswagen and putting it back together in the cafeteria."

"You deserved to be thrown out of school for that one. I heard she was terrified it would fall apart after that and finally wound up selling it for almost nothing."

His teeth captured her earlobe. "Mmmm," she sighed as his persistent nibbling sent a warmth throughout her body. "About the ceremony...." She leaned heavily against him as the effect of his teeth and tongue and breath reached her knees. "Would you mind if we were married here at the ranch—just us and Ben and the Edwardses?" She tilted her head to allow him freer access to her neck.

His tongue traced a fine moist line down the curving flesh from her ear to the base of her shoulder. "The townspeople will never forgive you." His voice sounded husky.

"They'll just assume we had to hurry things along and they'll patiently wait for the premature birth announcement. We'll have nine months before anyone realizes the truth and gets seriously testy. Certainly time enough to be forgiven for our impetuous behavior."

"If the story ever gets out that Russ came after me with a shotgun—"

"Perfect! I'll make sure Mavis Henry finds out. She'll take care of the rest of the county."

Steve turned her around to face him. "I will marry you anywhere, anytime you choose...in a submarine, a balloon, in front of a thousand people or just the two of us before God."

Her fingertips traced the outline of his jaw. A smile lit her eyes. "What I had in mind was a little less dramatic—sunrise in the Pine Nut Mountains."

He brought her hand to his mouth. "On the side of a very special hill where two lonely souls once found each other—"

"Where I first told you I loved you—"

"And where—"

"We first made love...."

He held her face between his hands. "Oh, my beautiful Danny...we've wasted so much time."

The stark pain in his voice made her flinch. "It's over," she soothed. "We've been through the worst that can come our way. Now it's our time for happiness." She breathed a kiss against his mouth. "Nothing bad can happen to us now...we have each other."

Their lips met in a fevered kiss, as if they could drive away all the pain they had known with the reality of a touch. The ache, the longing was immediately rekindled, and they were again at the same sharp point of needing each other that they had reached earlier, before Sean's arrival. Their acute awareness of each other drove out all but the loudest, most persistent noises of a ranch beginning another working day.

But those insistent sounds nudged Steve back into the real world, and he reluctantly broke the urgent contact of their bodies. "You don't want this to happen now, Danny," he said, his breath coming deeply.

"What?" She could not so readily return and had to use him to support her while her senses still reeled wildly.

"We can't make love now, not after what just happened in here. It will be too hard for you later. You'll spend all of next week being embarrassed in front of Ben and Russ instead of doing what has to be done."

"You're wrong!" But he couldn't have sobered her more quickly or more effectively with a bucket of ice water.

"Am I?" His eyes narrowed, challenging her to prove him wrong.

"For crying out loud, I'm a grown woman."

"You were a *woman* when I left." His hands dug emphatically into her shoulders. "I suppose you want me to believe that you've changed from a painfully circumspect pillar of your small-town community to a wildly sensuous creature who doesn't care who knows when she is engaged in a passion-filled tryst? It was one thing for everyone to see the car and speculate about what was happening in here between us three nights ago, quite another for them to know what two people who desperately want each other are obviously going to do when left alone."

Her shoulders sagged in defeat. "What makes you so . . . so . . . ."

"Intuitive? Or in control?"

"Either. Both!"

He sighed. After struggling for a moment in search of the proper words he finally, softly said, "Fear. If it didn't mean the jobs of several hundred people, I would never go back to New York without you. Leaving this place is going to be hard enough for you without spending the next week wondering if every sidelong glance has an extra meaning. I don't want you to go through that and I know you will if I stay here much longer." His lips pressed into her forehead with the softness of a falling autumn leaf.

Could he really be doing this? Was it possible he had told her it would be better if they didn't make love again? Steve found himself reaching for her, to pull her back into his arms when her quiet "thank you" stopped him.

"You're right about how I would feel facing Ben when you'd left," she said. "It's a stupid way to feel. I never felt guilty or embarrassed when we made love before...."

"Because we were always very careful. No one ever suspected."

"He's been like a father to me...."

Steve smiled and pinched the end of her nose. "I'm leaving before your opinion of how terrific I am gets a rude shock." He reached into his back pocket and withdrew a business card. "This is my work phone—" he took a pen from his shirt pocket and wrote a number across the back "—and this is my home phone number." He handed her the card. Their fingers touched, their eyes met; myriad silent messages were exchanged. Finally he pulled her to him and held her as he had dreamed he someday would. "I love you," he murmured against her mouth.

Several minutes later he was gone. As Danielle watched the rented car disappear down the long gravel driveway she saw Ben coming out of the barn. He grinned and waved before he went on with his work. Danielle reluctantly admitted again that Steve had been right—it would have been very difficult for her to face Ben had she and Steve spent the morning making love.

Irritated with herself and what she saw as unnecessary and archaic chains of morality, she walked back across the porch and slammed the kitchen door. She had been more sophisticated at sixteen.

Suddenly the enormity of what she was intending to do overcame her. She grabbed the sink and held on to it as if it were the only thing keeping her upright. Why had she ever said she would move to New York? What had ever made her think she could adapt to such an alien life? Ten years was a long time. Did they really love each other as they were now, or was it as they remembered?

Danielle looked down at the piece of paper in her hand. She stared at the name written there. Stephen Z. Maddox. Steve. She pressed the card to her chest and held it there until her breathing returned to normal.

She thought of the fearless child she had once been and chastised the weakling she had become. Determinedly she walked from the kitchen and up the stairs to her room to dress for the long day's work still ahead. Pausing to look from the bedroom window at the sprawling acres that made up the Double H Ranch, she fiercely reminded herself of her father's favorite homily—cowards die a thousand deaths, brave men die but once.

She had made her decision; she would not look back.

6

"THIS IS HOPELESS," Danielle wailed.

"It certainly is if you keep insisting everything has to get done this week." Ben leaned back in his chair, wearily rubbing his eyes. "It's not like you're leaving the planet," he said patiently. "There's none of this paperwork that can't be handled through the mail or over the phone. You don't have to finish it all before you leave."

She tossed her pencil on the table. "I can't shake the feeling that I'm skipping out and dumping all this on your shoulders." She waved her arm, indicating the table heaped with papers before them. "Not to mention the entire responsibility for running the ranch."

He reached for her hand. "My shoulders are broad enough to handle it. Beside, now that I know I'll have extra help to get me through this paper stuff, I think the job's gonna be easier on me than it ever was on you."

Danielle eyed him. "Oh? And just who, may I ask, is this extra help you are referring to?"

His face-splitting smile indicated he thought he had put one over on her. Rather smugly he said, "Russ told me Kathy worked as a bookkeeper before they were married." He shrugged nonchalantly. "I asked her if she was interested in a part-time job. She was real tickled, said it would be good to use her skills again." He was obviously immensely pleased with himself. "They're going to put aside what Kathy earns doing the books, for Sean's and Erica's college educations."

Danielle felt like she had stumbled onto the elaborate plans for a party—a party she hadn't been invited to. Intellectually it brought her a sense of comfort to know those around her were competently slipping into their new roles and that the ranch would continue to run smoothly without her; emotionally, it hurt more than she had lain awake nights imagining it would. "Have you decided who you're going to ask to take Russ's place?"

"Not yet. It would help if you'd stop being so stubborn about having me make my own choices and give me a clue as to who you'd like to see hired."

"If I were going to be around you know I would insist on approval, but there's a chance I'll never meet the man you hire, let alone have to work with him." She leaned forward, her elbows on the table, her chin resting in the cradle of her hands. "Have you consulted with Russ? Don't forget, now that he'll be taking over for you, the new man will be directly under him." Such reasonable, sensible words—then why did they hurt so much?

"Are you saying you're never planning on coming back?"

She left her chair and walked to the window. The sky overhead was black, fading to a deep purple over the distant peaks of the Sierra Nevadas. "I don't know. I've tried to imagine what my life will be like from now on...but I can't. Steve stayed away for ten years once, perhaps he won't ever want to come back."

"That doesn't mean you couldn't come. There are always vacations . . . holidays. . . ."

She turned to look at him, a thickening sheen of moisture making her eyes sparkle. "It's nice to hear that you're going to miss me. Ever since Steve returned I've felt like I had your hand in the small of my back pushing me out the door."

"Maybe it has been," he admitted. "But it's been for your own good. I certainly never intended for you to get the idea you weren't ever to come back here though." His voice grew louder. "You best remember that those kids you two are going to have can't develop a love for a place they never see."

A tiny smile that was as much a prelude to tears as an assurance made the corners of her mouth twitch. "I'll remember," she promised.

STEVE APPEARED two nights later, arriving an hour early for the wedding feast Kathy Edwards had spent the day preparing. Ben, Danielle, Steve and the Edwardses stuffed themselves on barbecued ribs, corn on the cob, fresh-baked bread and German potato salad. By the time cake and homemade ice cream had been served they were groaning at their collective gluttony.

The early evening gently turned into the twilight hour, which came and went in warm conversation and remembrances, bonding old ties between Steve, Danielle and Ben, and establishing new ones that included the Edwardses. More than once Danielle mentally pulled away from this small gathering of people she loved above all others and fervently wished that Steve had come to stay, not to take her away.

The day of the wedding arrived with the hushed quality of a lover's contented sigh. Alone in her room in the darkness of early morning, hours before she had to get ready, Danielle took her grandmother's wedding dress from the closet and with trembling hands laid it gently across the bed. She wondered briefly what the staunch traditionalists among her friends would say when they heard of her decision to wear the gown she should have worn at her first wedding. She considered the question as she ran her hand over the rich satin. Straightening a folded piece of lace, she realized that those of her friends who even gave the dress a second thought would know why she had not worn it before, why she had saved it to wear when she married Steve.

The satin and lace had turned a soft ivory and deep ecru, making her job of matching material to lengthen the sleeves and hem harder than she had anticipated. Alone in her room all night, after all other work had been done, she had lovingly sewn new lace on the gown. Now the dress lay waiting for her.

She turned from the bed to her dressing table. The special care she had taken with her hair the previous night, thoroughly drying it before going to bed so that she would not awaken with any wild surprises, had paid off. She needed only to bush the sleep-tangled curls until they lay smoothly against her back in soft glistening waves. As she ran the brush through her hair, the sun-streaked strands picked up and reflected the light from her lamp, making the soft brown mass seem shot with gold. When she was satisfied that it looked as good as she could make it, she pulled the sides back and held them with a tortoiseshell clip, then added tiny sprigs of fresh baby's breath.

Out of habit she wore no jewelry. Her face she enhanced with only a touch of lipstick, her long mink-colored lashes providing a natural frame for eyes her father had once called prettier than the cornflower blue of his brand new Pontiac. Quite a compliment from a man who had treated his car with only a modicum less love and attention than he'd treated his wife.

With precise movements she finished getting ready, realizing that each step of the process was in a way, a celebration as well as a preparation for farewell. When at last she stood at the doorway she paused only an instant before reaching for the switch and plunging the room into darkness.

Her steps down the stairs were slow, her actions unhurried. She had purposely planned this hour. It was a private time, a time to say goodbye to the only home she had ever known. Wandering from room to room, she no longer fought the memories. Instead she let them wash over her, revelling in the good and the bad, the sad and the happy, heavyhearted on this day only because her brother and her parents could not witness her happiness.

By the time Ben arrived, she was ready—in every way—to begin her new life.

STEVE STOOD ON a flat rock on the side of a hill, watching the headlights grow larger as Danielle's truck approached. His tuxedo jacket open, his hands thrust into his pant pockets, he was unaware of the coldness of the early morning or the soft voices of the people standing behind him. He took deep calming breaths of the sage-scented air as he listened to the sound of his heart pounding heavily in his ears. All week he had fought a euphoria that had made him grin broadly at the worst possible times during highly critical budget meetings, whistle crazy tunes in elevators, and walk from room to room in his apartment in a daze of confusion, not knowing why he had begun to wander in the first place. A pervasive alien superstition had shadowed his every thought and action: he must not celebrate too soon. If he did, the reason for celebration might disappear as easily as did foolish promises made in the throes of passion.

"Almost," he breathed, urging the truck's headlights to grow larger. Just one more hour and the dream he had been too fearful to allow himself to dream this past week would finally be his. "Come to me, my beautiful Danny," he whispered. "Be mine today, be mine for always." In his pocket he felt the ring he had bought for her, his thumb rubbing it as though it were a worry stone.

Finally the truck stopped at the base of the hill. Unconsciously Steve held his breath as he waited, still unable to trust that what he had wanted for so long was about to come true. Ben walked around the truck, opened the door.... Danny appeared, an apparition in soft white. He had always thought her beautiful, but today she destroyed the memory of every other woman he had ever seen. He ached to go to her but could not move.

DANIELLE WASN'T SURE when it was she first spotted Steve standing on the side of the hill looking like a lonely sentinel as he waited for her; she only knew that once she had seen him she could look nowhere else. She smiled with a secret, profound pleasure when they drew close enough for her to see that he had dressed formally, as if they were to be married in a cathedral instead of on a desert mountain.

As she watched him, the last of Danielle's fears and doubts slipped from her mind as easily, as completely as winter snows disappear in spring. *I love you, Stephen Zackery Maddox*, she silently told him, never doubting that he could hear her. *I promise you that from this day on we will be together, always.*

The truck stopped. She saw his love for her shining from his eyes—love so powerful it was like a beacon to guide her final steps.

Just as the sun broke above the horizon, they spoke their vows. There were tears. There was laughter. Embraces replaced words of love from those who could express them no other way.

Ben insisted they all have one final meal together, saying he would cook everyone breakfast. The gathering was a celebration tinged with sadness. Later when it was time for her and Steve to leave, someone asked Danielle if she knew what she had eaten. Sheepishly she had to admit she didn't.

As he kissed her goodbye a disgruntled-sounding Ben loudly vowed he would never cook for her again, swearing he would find someone who appreciated his kitchen talents before he could be persuaded to put pancake to griddle for them. And then whispering so that only she could hear, he told her he would cook every meal when she came "home" for a visit.

They all waved farewell until not even an arm swinging high in the air could be seen. Finally Danielle turned to face the front of the car. A lone tear worked its way down her cheek to land inconspicuously on her soft blue linen suit.

Steve reached over to wipe the traces of the tear from her cheek. He placed his hand over hers, curling his fingers so that they rested against her palm. "Scared?" he queried.

"No. Well, a little, I guess."

"Me too."

The emotional storm that had controlled her as if she were caught in the funnel of a rampaging tornado suddenly lost its force and she felt at peace for the first time in weeks. With the disappearance of the storm her natural pervasive sense of humor returned. She glanced at Steve and saw how hard the time had been on him, too. As if giving him reassurance she closed her hand, squeezing his fingers lightly. Her eyes twinkling mischievously, she said, "Don't worry, Steve. I'll be gentle."

He groaned. "Dammit, Danny, stop that. If you only knew what talk like that from you does to me. I've been going out of my mind this past week with wanting you."

She wriggled closer. Tugging her hand from his, she placed it familiarly on his thigh. "What makes you think I haven't been suffering the same frustrations?" Her voice had dropped to a seductive whisper.

"You wouldn't be doing what you're doing now if you really understood what I've been going through."

"Is that right? I suppose you think only men have those feelings, huh?" Her finger traced the crisp pleat of his tan slacks, slowly traveling upward from his knee. Before she was at mid-thigh his hand clasped hers, stopping her from going any farther.

"You should have told me earlier that you wanted to make love on a bed of sand one last time," he said evenly. "I would have brought along a blanket. As it is, we'll just have to try to find a spot that will be a little less rough on your backside than the usual fare."

"Surely you jest," she said in mock horror. "Why, my new suit would be ruined—not to mention my fancy coiffure. I'm shocked, sir, that you should even suggest such a thing." She touched her hair, which she'd pinned up in a coil, as if seeking a stray strand. "You couldn't possibly be trying to tell me, now that it's too late for me to do anything about it, that you're one of those . . . those . . . *lusty* types, are you?"

"No, not exactly—"

"Damn," she pouted. "I was so hoping. . . ." She eyed him indignantly. "And who said anything about *me* being on the bottom?"

Steve laughed aloud. It was a wonderfully happy sound, one that marked the release of the incredible tension he had been under for so long. "How could I have forgotten what a minx you can be?" he said, bringing her hand to his lips for a quick kiss.

She snuggled against him. Serious again, she said, "What fun we're going to have rediscovering all the little things about each other we've forgotten over the years."

"And perhaps finding out one or two new things in the process," he said, an air of mystery about him.

"Are you trying to tell me something?"

He waited for long suspenseful moments, then, in an agonized voice, said, "I probably should have mentioned this before now . . . but I'm sure once I tell you what I have to say, you'll understand why I didn't—why I couldn't." He paused dramatically. "My appetite, my tastes, about certain, uh, *things* have changed since the last time we, uh, the last time we...." He shrugged. "I'm sorry, Danny. I don't know how to tell you this. More than anything else, this separates the person I was when I left here from the person I am now."

"For heaven's sake, just spit it out!" His words were so hesitant, so tortured that a feeling of unease had begun to settle over her.

"First of all, it's important for me that you know how desperately I fought it...for years I fought it. The whole idea seemed repugnant, almost sick in a way. But finally, about three or four years ago, when I realized how odd it made me look to constantly avoid what everyone else in my circle of friends considered the ultimate pleasure, I gave in." Impatiently he brushed the hair from his forehead.

"I started out slow," he continued. "I had decided the best way to handle it was to build my tolerance over the span of several parties. Then one day I was stunned to discover I had started enjoying it—actually found myself seeking it out. I even began indulging when I was alone in my apartment." Again he paused. "I'm afraid I'm hooked, Danny," he quietly confessed.

She swallowed, trying to dislodge the lump in her throat. She had read such horrible stories of the things that went on in well-to-do circles. "Whatever it is, Steve, we can—"

He didn't wait for her reassurances, finishing his agonized confession as if he was unaware she'd begun to speak. "After years of fighting it . . . I find I actually *like* caviar."

It took a stunned instant to register, but when Danielle realized that she had gone after his bait like a hungry large-mouth bass after a fat nightcrawler, she chewed her lip to keep from laughing. When she was sure she could handle it she tilted her face toward him, gave him the most serious look she could muster and innocently asked, "Spread where?"

His sharp intake of breath made it impossible to refrain from smiling. She stared at him through hooded, sultry eyes. "Still want to play word games?"

He recovered quickly. "Would you really like to hear what kind of games I had envisioned for us?"

The core of warmth that sent heat radiating through her midsection reminded her she was not as much in control as she pretended to be. "Why don't you surprise me?"

"Now?" he asked, obviously willing to accommodate her should she ask.

She feigned a yawn. "I can wait."

Again she heard the marvelous sound of his laughter. How beautiful her world was this morning.

DANIELLE LOOKED CLOSELY at already familiar sights as they drove past the state capitol building on their way through Carson City to the airport on the northeast side of town.

Steve had noted the growing silences between them as they neared the town, and respecting what he assumed were the reasons, had not tried to fill them with conversation. Despite all that had happened he felt they continued to inhabit a fragile world. He wouldn't, he couldn't allow himself to fully believe the events of that morning until he and Danny had left Nevada far behind them. A phrase kept echoing in his mind—*it's just too damn good to be true*. He couldn't shake the feeling that someone didn't dream what was seemingly an impossible dream for ten years and wake up one morning to discover that in the space of less than three weeks the dream had come true.

As if reading his thoughts, Danielle reached toward his leg, touching him with a reassurance that was like a thick wool blanket on the cold fear that insisted on lingering around his heart. Sunlight framed her hand, and her ring sent spectrums of brilliant color dancing across the dashboard. Slowly she moved her finger, watching as the spots filled the car. "It's beautiful, Steve," she said, admiring the single large yellow stone centered between two wide bands. "I've never seen anything like it before—what is it?"

"It's a diamond. The salesman at Cartier's called it canary yellow. When I went out shopping I only knew I wanted something unusual, something special. When he showed me this one, I thought the color seemed a good one for you."

Danielle didn't know what to say. She knew nothing about jewelry, but had sense enough to know the ring must have cost a fortune. "Can we afford this?" she finally stammered.

The "we" pleased him; the subtle reminder of how little she knew the man he had become sent a warning chill down his spine. It wasn't that she had ever known poverty, or had ever been denied by her parents any reasonable request when growing up; in fact, she was undoubtedly a millionaire in her own right should her paper assets be tallied. Yet her life had been lived in a sheltered, genteel environment where material trappings were considered ostentatious if not in downright bad taste.

"Would it bother you a great deal if I told you yes, we can afford your ring?" Before she could answer, he went on, "I suppose now that we're discussing this I should also tell you that we live in a nice apartment."

"You've been successful, then."

Never before had he felt apologetic about the amount of money he made. "Eagle Enterprises does okay," he hedged.

She looked again at the splendid stone sparkling with its own life on her hand. It suddenly felt very heavy. How did someone rich act? "Boy..." she sighed, determined not to let him know how his news had effected her. "First caviar, and now this." She gave him a tentative smile. "I guess all in all, it's better than being poor and starving."

He put his arm around her, pulled her to him and placed a quick kiss on her temple. "You might say that." He smiled in pleasure.

A short time later they were at the airport terminal returning the rental car. Slipping his plastic identification card back into his wallet, Steve turned and took Danielle's arm. "Ready?"

She nodded, wondering if he suspected this would be the first time she had flown in anything larger than her father's Piper Cub. Steve gathered her single suitcase and his garment bag and indicated they were to exit from a side door.

The pneumatic door was still hissing closed when Danielle spotted a grinning silver-haired man plainly headed their way.

"Mr. Maddox!" he said cheerfully in greeting. His smile broadened as he came close enough to reach for the luggage; his eyes never left Danielle. "Everything is ready...."

"Jerry, I suppose I should tell you that the beautiful woman you're ogling happens to be my wife, Danielle Hart—" He stopped and looked into her eyes, and it was as if only at that moment did all that had transpired before become real. "Danielle Maddox." The pride was unmistakable.

"Danny, this incredibly contrary and independent individual I sometimes laughingly refer to as an employee is Jerry Wainwright."

Jerry took her hand, but instead of shaking it briefly, the action she had anticipated upon a normal introduction, he held on to it in a touchingly courtly manner. "I didn't think he had it in him," he said. "Steve's had some real lookers before but you're the first one of substance he's ever brought to the plane. I don't mind telling you I was a little leery when he told me what he was doing back here." His eyes sparkled merrily as he kissed her cheek. "Congratulations. He's a hell of a guy—but then I can see right off that he's gotten himself one hell of a woman."

"Thank you," she said, struggling to meet his overwhelming personality head on. "For both . . . for everything."

He looked at Steve. "We're all set to go as soon as you say."

Steve looked questioningly at Danielle.

"Yes. I'm ready," she said softly.

But it wasn't to the commercial airliner they walked. It was to a sleek silver Learjet with a stylistic eagle poised on the tail section. Danielle turned questioning eyes to Steve.

He shrugged. "It's the company plane."

"And Jerry?"

"The pilot."

Slowly shaking her head she again looked at the plane. "Sometime this next week you're going to have to fill me in on just exactly what it is you do for a living." They walked a little farther. "It is legal, isn't it?" she whispered.

Steve's laughter brought a quizzical glance from Jerry.

"The lady was simply questioning the way I do business," Steve explained.

"He's the tops, Mrs. Maddox. I know some people who have even named children after him." He grinned. "And not for the usual reasons either."

"Are you going to tell her about the ones who would like to see my head on a platter, too?" Steve asked.

"Aw, you can't seriously consider them. No one likes losing a job."

"People lose their jobs because of you?" she asked.

Steve guided her up the stairs. "It's a long story. I'll tell you about it later."

Once inside Danielle stopped and gaped. This wasn't a plane, it was a luxurious airborne office complete with wet bar and paintings on the oak-panelled walls. She felt Steve's hand give her a gentle nudge. "Would it be all right if I come in?"

"I suppose so," she mumbled absently as she stepped out of the doorway.

Steve nervously brushed back the hair from his forehead. What yesterday had simply been a comfortable company airplane in which he spent a great deal of time, suddenly had become an overwhelmingly flagrant expression of wealth. It was as if he were seeing the richly upholstered furniture, original artwork and thick carpeting for the first time because he was seeing it with Danny—someone who still kept her grandmother's hand crocheted antimacassars on the backs of her sofas and chairs.

"It's lovely," she finally said. And then, under her breath, added, "Certainly a step or two above my father's Piper Cub."

Steve hadn't realized he had been holding his breath until he released it in a long heavy sigh. "I'm glad you like it." He gave the generic reply easily, as if it held only the standard meaning.

When the last-minute preparations for their flight had been finished, Steve led Danielle to a chair and helped her with the seat belt. It seemed only minutes after they had been speeding along the runway that they were looking down at Carson City and then the Double H Ranch. Danielle closed her eyes, whispered a last goodbye to the people, the land she loved and turned resolutely from the window. She tucked her arm in Steve's and leaned against his shoulder. "We did it."

He pressed his lips to the top of her head, breathing in the clean herbal scent. "After what had to be the world's record detour."

"Have you ever wondered if maybe it was best that it happened this way?"

"Meaning?" he queried.

"Perhaps we weren't ready...."

"Yes, I've thought about that. Looking back to the person I was then and comparing that man to the one I am now, I know I am freer now to give you my love and to accept yours in return. The man I remember was filled with desperation, frantically trying to run away from so many things...." His voice trailed off.

Danielle was afraid to move, afraid to breathe; she sensed he was about to tell her what phantoms had been his companions for so many years, something he had relentlessly refused to share with her before. She could almost feel from the tenseness of his arm the internal war he waged. Long seconds passed. She waited. The moment slipped away. Steve's arm perceptibly relaxed. Obviously he had decided there were certain doors that should remain closed between them awhile longer. Danielle was acutely disappointed but willing to wait, knowing someday the time would be right.

Steve unhooked his seat belt, then reached over to remove Danielle's. "Do you want anything? Something to eat? Drink?"

"What would you say if I told you that the only thing I wanted was you?" she asked.

He kissed her lightly on the tip of the nose. "Do you have any particular preferences? Vertical? Horizontal perhaps?" He grinned mischievously. "How about supine on that nice big sofa over there?"

"Add au natural and you're beginning to get the idea."

"Danny, my love," he chuckled, "you astonish me. Would you really engage in a little tryst with our pilot only one thin door away?"

"He's busy. He can't come in here," she reasoned. "Who would fly the plane?"

"Ever heard of automatic pilot?" He could tell by her surprised expression that the thought had not occurred to her.

"He wouldn't . . . would he?"

Steve stood and reached for her, pulling her into his arms. "No, he wouldn't. But that still doesn't make it a very good idea."

She sighed heavily. "Isn't it the bride who's supposed to be reluctant? Have I lost my sex appeal or something?"

"Do I hear a challenge?" he said in a deceptively calm voice.

"What you hear is a highly frustrated female."

He breathed a kiss on the sensitive hollow at the base of her ear. "How much of that frustration do you think we could eliminate in thirty minutes?"

She moved her head, urging him to continue to explore her neck. "I had no idea we would be making love on a timetable."

"Making love, no. Flying, yes." He undid the top button of her blouse. "But then I suppose I could ask Jerry to circle the airport for a couple of hours...."

She hesitated, as if giving the idea serious consideration. "Do we have enough fuel?" She could feel a chuckle vibrate his chest.

He was still smiling when he led her to the sofa and pulled her down beside him. "*Nothing* is going to interfere or distract us when we make love for the first time as man and wife." He ran the back of his hand lightly across her breast. "I want at least ten uninterrupted hours."

Danielle slipped out of her heels. "Is that all?" With a fluid, sensual movement she swung her legs up and laid them on the rich brocade, then leaned back across

Steve's lap. "If we're not going to play around, why don't you tell me why you make people lose their jobs."

"Now? Wouldn't you rather hear me mumble words of endearment?"

Her manner was serious when she answered. "I want to know everything about you—your job, your plans, your hopes and dreams—even any more grotesque eating habits you've acquired over the years." She laced her fingers through his where they lay below her breast.

"My dreams have come true; my hopes are all for our future together." His hand tightened its hold on hers. "I'm not so foolish that I think our life will be easy. It's going to be terribly hard on you. If there were only some way...."

With her free hand she reached up and pressed a finger to his lips. "I know ... but let's not prejudge or try to guess what kind of problems face us. We're liable to invent a few that would never have existed otherwise." She smiled encouragingly. "Now tell me about Eagle Enterprises."

He settled deeper into the sofa and leaned his head back. "After I dropped out of college," he began, "I took what little money I had set aside and began investing in real estate. That was back when property sometimes doubled in a month—when some mornings a home could go on the market for $100,000 and after an auction that afternoon, sell for $150,000.

"I started coming across poorly operated companies that were being sold for the market value of the buildings. On a lark one day I decided to see if I could turn one of those companies around." He smiled at the memory. "It was the most incredible feeling of accomplishment—like being given a complex mental puzzle to take apart and put back together properly, a puzzle that had real risks and frequently involved very high stakes."

"And the people who loved you and named their children after you?"

"They were the owners I'd saved from financial ruin—the people who kept their jobs because the company stayed afloat."

"And the ones who lost their jobs?"

"Were the men and women, usually at the executive level, who simply weren't needed. Contrary to popular belief, excess employees are usually at the top of the company, not the rank and file."

His animation, his enthusiasm, the sparkle in his eyes revealed as much to Danielle as his words. "And Eagle Enterprises?" she prodded.

"Eagle is a small group of extremely capable men and women who get as big a charge out of turning companies around as I do. They work in teams—I'm what you might call a floating coach. I decide, after a thorough investigation, which troubled companies are basically sound. When we've taken one on as a client, we ready a team, send it in with absolute authority to make the changes we deem necessary. At the end of a period of time, usually two or three years, sometimes only one, we utilize the stock options given to us in the beginning. Needless to say, by then the stock has become quite valuable. Everyone on the team gets a percentage."

"You make it sound so easy."

Steve smiled as he smoothed his hand over her hair. "You'd be amazed at how easy it can be sometimes. Of course, as I mentioned before, we're either loved or hated; there's nothing in between."

"I can see the reasoning behind that." She gave him an innocent look. "But then I can't imagine ever feeling neutral toward you."

He traced the outline of her ear with his fingertip. "What can you imagine feeling?"

"Right now?" When he nodded, she answered, "What I'm feeling right this very minute is pure, unadulterated lust."

"Mmmm . . . you always did have a marvelous way with words."

"You think that's good," she said, a beguiling look in her eyes. "You should see what I can do with my—"

"Enough, Danielle!"

She smiled in satisfaction at his use of her full name. Slipping her hand behind his neck, she pulled him to her. Pliant, warm lips met, melded, opened. Tongues caressed, teased, thrust. Danielle moaned her desire, so quickly and fiercely rekindled. Steve lifted her, bringing her more completely into his arms.

"Enough?" she breathed. "Will we ever have enough of each other?"

"Once we get to Monterey," he vowed, "I intend to give it one hell of a try."

A soft chime sounded in the background. Steve turned to look out the window. "Would you like to take your first look at the Pacific Ocean?"

Danielle had her nose pressed snugly to the glass before she realized it was double paned. Her mouth formed a silent "O." They were passing over a patchwork of farmland, a quilt seemingly composed of every conceivable shade of green.

Mountains covered with wild grasses baked to an early summer gold edged the verdant fields. Her eyes quickly passed over the hills and the long fertile Salinas Valley, then traveled to the wide expanse of blue to the west. To someone whose entire life had been spent surrounded by shades of brown and the deep green of piñon pines, the scene before her had an eerie sense of unreality—as if she had been suspended above a garishly painted canvas. "It's beautiful...." The awe in her voice was that of a child's on Christmas morning.

The plane banked. Steve took her hand and led her back to the seats they had occupied on takeoff. He hooked her seat belt and pulled it snugly across her hips. Touching her chin, he turned her to face him. His mouth tenderly brushed over hers. "There are so many things I want to show you—to share with you."

She leaned against his shoulder. "Remind me every once in a while not to stand around with my mouth open while you're showing me these things. I don't want to become known as the human flycatcher."

7

DANIELLE STEPPED from the plane into the brilliant noon sunshine. She stopped to inhale more deeply the oddly scented, moisture-laden air. "Steve," she said. "What is that strange smell?"

"That fine odor, my dear, is the result of millions of gallons of sea water beating against a rocky shoreline. Like it?"

Her eyes widened. "It always smells like this?"

"Always."

"I suppose you get used to it after a while?"

"Some people have even been known to grow to like it."

"Funny," she said, disbelief evident in her tone. "I remember reading that the Monterey area had several old missions, but I don't remember reading anything about miracles."

He took her arm. "I promise you, you'll feel differently by the end of the week."

She glanced at him. "Cross your heart and hope to die, stick a needle in—"

"Cross my heart, you can have. The rest you can forget."

She buried her nose in his jacket sleeve and mumbled something unintelligible into the blue serge.

"Try breathing through your mouth," he suggested.

Her glance became a frown. "I can tell you're not taking this very seriously." She sounded as if she had suddenly come down with pneumonia. "Do you have any idea how traumatic it could be for someone to discover they had chosen a place to spend their honeymoon that made them gag?"

He bent his head to whisper in her ear. "I'll make you another promise. In approximately half an hour your senses will be too busy with other distractions for you to even care where you are or what it smells like."

She smiled. "Oh, I like your style, Maddox."

The drive from the airport took slightly longer than the thirty minutes Steve had predicted. He hadn't known how long it would take to register at the entrance gate to the Seventeen Mile drive where Eagle Enterprises owned a home—a bonus given the company by a particularly grateful client four years earlier. With the famed Pebble Beach Golf Club next door, the house was frequently used for both pleasure and business by the dozen or so golfing fanatics who worked for Eagle Enterprises. Having no interest in golf and no time for hobbies, Steve had never been there.

As they drove the meandering road across land

some had called the most spectacular on earth, Danielle silently stared at the blue-on-blue horizon. Occasionally her gaze shifted to the rocky shoreline, where every few minutes or so a wave would leap magnificently high.

Clustered beside the road and in the hills were lovely homes reminiscent of those Danielle had seen in the nicest areas of Reno. Steve, acting as tour guide and repeating information he had learned from people at the office, told her they were passing through the most recently developed section of the private community. He added that the old homes, which had once been owned by Hollywood moguls in the thirties and forties, were located closer to Carmel.

Danielle shrugged expressively. "Beautiful seems so meaningless," she said.

"I understand," he answered, reaching for her hand. "I feel that way when I look at you."

It was as if his words had burst the tiny pod of warmth she carried locked in her chest. "You know, Steve...." She struggled for the right words. "I'm not...." She had tried to relegate to the back of her mind the fragmented fears that he would not find her body as attractive as he once had, yet like spiders to corners the fears insisted on returning. "You know, I'm not the 'girl' you once made love to. My body has changed...."

If it hadn't been for the hesitant pained way she had spoken her fears he would have given in to his first instinct and laughed. He thought about the night she had sat across from him completely encased in an old chenille bathrobe and how his heart had raced and how the fire had burned in his loins. He thought of the curving swell of her hips in snug-fitting jeans, the way the feel of her unyielding breasts pressed against his own unyielding chest made his senses celebrate the differences between them, the soft wisps of hair that lay against the nape of her neck, the hint of old-fashioned lavender that surrounded her like an elusive memory.

"If you honestly believe it makes any difference to me how firm or thin or rounded you are," he said, "what do you think is going to happen to us twenty years from now?"

"It's just that—"

"Danny, when I say I love you, it isn't the span of your waist or the fullness of your breasts I'm talking about." He grinned. "As a matter of fact, I'm looking forward to the day when your waistline disappears and your breasts are temporarily used for their intended function. Do you honestly believe I would love you less then?"

"Give me time. Everything has happened so fast." She looked up and noticed they were passing a broad expanse of meticulously tended grass that abutted the ocean. "Oh, by the way, you probably should turn around the next chance you get," she said. "We passed number 54 at the last curve."

"Why didn't you say something?"

"And stop you from saying what you were saying? Fat chance. I would have let you drive on to San Francisco before I'd do that."

"For future reference, we happen to be headed in the direction of Los Angeles." Steve turned around in the parking lot of the Pebble Beach Lodge. As he approached the house he swung off the main road, where they were stopped by a ten-foot-high ornamental iron gate blocking the entrance to number 54 Ocean Front Drive. Withdrawing an electronic key from his jacket, he inserted it into the lock and the gate swung open. The driveway that led through windswept pines offered the pair only glimpses of the house. When the pines gave way to a broad opening, the building was at last revealed in all its splendor.

Danielle had never imagined anything so grand. Redwood and rock and glass had been expertly combined to create a house perfectly in harmony with its natural surroundings. Steve reached over and gently closed Danielle's mouth. "Flies, remember?"

"You own this?" It was an odd combination of question and accusation.

"Eagle Enterprises owns it. The company also owns a condominium in Sun Valley and an apartment in New Orleans. We use them as tax write-offs."

Staring again at the house she said, "Just how rich are you?"

"Does it matter?"

She looked at the surrounding land and instinctively knew it was worth two or three times the price of the house. Thoughtfully she chewed her lower lip. "Whenever I had to spend more than a day in Reno I would take an hour or two and watch the high rollers playing the tables. Money passed through their hands as if there were an endless supply. I used to wonder what they were really like—they seemed so different from anyone I knew, so apart from my experiences. I stopped watching them a few years back when the economy started going downhill and people all over had to struggle for their next meal."

"Just because I've been successful, you're equating them with me? Don't you see how unfair you're being?" The frustration, the anger were unmistakable.

Tearing her gaze from the house she sighed. "I don't know what I'm doing." Suddenly a tiny piece of lint on her lap demanded all of her attention. "I used to walk on such firm ground. These last few weeks I feel as though I've been suspended in air, and I seem to be constantly groping for something solid to hang on to."

Steve touched her cheek with the back of his hand. "I wish I could help you."

"I feel so foolish." She tried to smile. "Cinderella had it more together than I do."

"I'm sure if you had a wicked stepmother at home, leaving would have been far easier."

Her mouth curved into a real smile. "I love you."

He took her hand. "Come on. Let's look around."

Before going into the house they walked across the lawn toward the ocean. Danielle was delighted to find a stairway leading down to a tiny beach at the base of the rocks. Halfway down the stairs Steve abruptly turned and demanded, "Breathe deeply."

Startled, she complied.

"Well?"

Understanding dawned. Reluctantly she admitted, "I like it."

His hands went to her waist. With Danielle standing one step higher on the stairs they were at eye level. "Remember this, Danny. Just because something is new or different or possibly even unpleasant at first doesn't mean it's necessarily bad." He measured his words carefully, knowing he walked a fine line between asking her to understand what he was trying to tell her and preaching. "Because of you I've begun to feel guilty that I've been successful—as if I should apologize to you for having had the audacity to do well." His voice became a plea. "Don't do that to me, Danny."

"I'm sorry. I didn't realize...."

He brushed the windblown hair from her eyes. Gently their lips touched and tasted. "Come on," he said, turning to finish walking down the stairs. When they were both on the sand he told her, "Take off your shoes."

"And my stockings?"

He grinned lasciviously. "I'll do that."

"Oh no, you won't. You're not coming near me. I'll take them off myself. I've made love on sand for the last time. From now on, it's a bed or nothing."

"No sofas?"

She hesitated, as if seriously considering the possibility. "I suppose under the proper circumstances I could be persuaded—" she stepped out of her shoes "—to deviate from my future pattern...." Quickly looking around to reassure herself that they were still alone, Danielle slid her skirt up the length of her thighs and hooked her thumbs in the elastic band of her pantyhose. "Should the proper persuasion—" in a lithe, graceful movement she stripped the hose from her legs "—be applied." She crossed the sand to where Steve stood and leisurely began stuffing the sheer nylon into his pocket.

"Such as?" he asked.

"You've forgotten?" she breathed, opening his jacket and snuggling against the warmth of his chest.

"I may need an extensive refresher course." He wrapped his jacket around her.

"I can recommend a great teacher." She pressed her lips to his neck in furtive kisses.

"Anyone I know?"

"Possibly."

"If not, I'm sure there are good books on the subject at the library," he said.

"Trust me. This has to be a hands-on learning experience."

"Trust you? Shall I tell you what happened to me the last time a woman said 'trust me'? And in my own apartment, no less."

Danielle leaned her head back and looked at him through hooded eyes. "No, don't tell me. I don't want to know."

Steve gave a small deprecatory snort. "Ha—no guts."

"All right, all right, what happened?"

"I wound up with five cases of assorted household brushes."

Danielle laughed. "That's not true, is it?"

"Every word."

Again she laughed. "What did you do with them?"

"I'll let that be a surprise." He took her hand. "Just be careful opening the closets when we get home."

Steve led her to the water's edge, where the sand was cold and packed as hard as the sand at the ranch. He, too, was now barefoot, and his pants were rolled up. The next wave was stronger than the last and Danielle watched with wide eyes as the foaming sheet of water sped toward them. She started to back up but Steve held her. When the wave covered her feet and rose above her ankles she gasped in surprise. It was so cold!

"People swim in here? This is where Surf City and the Beach Boys came from?" she choked.

"You're about three hundred miles north of all that. This area is known more for its beauty than its water sports, but it's my understanding that some people do go swimming here."

Steve watched her, glorying in, sharing in, each of her discoveries as they explored the tiny beach. He smiled in pleasure when she grew braver and stepped closer to meet the incoming waves. This time together was so very important. It was critical for them both that she have new experiences that had nothing to do with the ranch.

Brutally he forced himself to admit that it was probably more important to him than her. He had to find a way to hold on to her, to keep her beside him always. The longer they were together, the more evident it became that his life had been irrevocably changed the day he'd returned to Nevada. He could not go back to the way it had been before. How incongruous that a woman who looked as fragile as a dandelion had, without conscious effort or guile, instilled in him a sense of hesitancy and caution—traits previously as alien to him as love had been.

"Why so quiet?" Danielle asked, shattering his reverie.

"What?" He blinked his eyes, trying to focus. Danielle had come up beside him, her hands filled with shells. The wind had all but unpinned her hair. It blew wild and free, long gleaming strands of golden-brown silk. Her suit jacket was spotted with salt water and sand, the hem of her skirt held a solid dark ring where a wave had surprised her. She was smiling, wearing her contentment and happiness like a shiny new necklace.

"I was just thinking," he said, taking the shells from her hands and carefully putting them in his pockets, "I'm getting awfully hungry."

"Me, too." She brushed the sand from her suit, then turned and headed for the stairs. Hesitating at the first step, she looked back over her shoulder and asked, "Got any caviar?"

The corners of his mouth twitched with the beginning of a smile. "I'm sure there must be at least one jar. I sent word ahead to have the kitchen stocked." He started to follow her. "However, I'm not sure about crackers."

"Come on, Maddox," she scolded softly, "be creative."

He paused a moment as if giving her suggestion serious careful consideration. "Well, I can see a few possibilities."

"Awrrr . . ." she growled in frustration.

Steve winked at her. With precise deliberate movements he touched the end of his finger to the tip of his tongue and made an invisible mark in the air. The way he figured it, they were even.

When they reached the house Steve unlocked the door with the same key he had used to open the front gate. Danielle peered inside. A slate-tiled foyer as big as her living room at the ranch shone back in gleaming splendor. "We can't go in there like this," Danielle said in a hushed whisper. "Isn't there a back porch or at least someplace that won't show every footprint and every grain of sand we drag in?"

"It's highly unlikely," he answered in normal tones. "But I'll check it out if you want me to."

"No." She put her hand on his arm. "Wait."

Before he realized what she intended to do, Danielle had stepped out of her skirt and started unbuttoning her jacket. As Steve watched her he leaned against the doorframe, one hand resting comfortably on his hip. When she had her jacket, blouse and slip neatly folded on top of her skirt and was left standing in only her bikini pants and bra he grinned appreciatively and said, "Just what makes you think we're alone?"

Danielle grabbed her clothes and jumped from the doorway. "Who's here?" she gasped.

"Well, there could be a maid or a cook—a gardener certainly wouldn't be out of the question." He was having a hard time keeping a smile from his face. When he had decided she had had enough, he said, "But you're in luck. I left explicit instructions that we were to be left alone."

She threw her neatly folded clothing at him. "You rat!"

When he looked up again from gathering the scattered clothing she was gone. Quickly he removed his own jacket, shirt and slacks and followed. He found a subdued Danielle in the living room repinning her hair, framed by a wall of windows that faced the ocean. Standing as she was with her arms raised and backlit by the sun reflecting off the ocean, she seemed a magnificent work of art. Steve dropped the bundle of clothes he carried onto the tile floor in the hallway. Coming up behind her, he slipped his arms around her waist and pressed a kiss to the curve of her shoulder. "You deserved that," he said.

"Oh?" She felt his kiss as keenly in the pit of her stomach as at the base of her neck.

"The skirt I could understand—maybe even the jacket. But the slip and blouse?"

His bare skin felt warm and good against her own. "You know how it is once you get started," she said.

Gently his hand began kneading the smooth flesh of her belly. "No," he said, his breath a hot caress on her back, "tell me how it is once you get started." His hands moved higher to brush against the keenly receptive undersides of her breasts as he lovingly outlined the curve of bone where her ribs joined. Following the line upward he came to her bra. A moment later the material had been brushed aside and her breasts were free. Her nerve endings seemed exposed, unprotected, so acutely attuned to his loving tender strokes that the pleasure she experienced bordered on pain. When at last he captured and massaged the passion-hardened nipples between thumb and forefinger she caught her breath. A surge of intense wanting radiated through her midsection.

She startled to turn but he held her closer, forcing her to stay as she was. His tongue circled the outside of her ear, then possessively invaded the sensitive interior as he held her even more firmly against him. Adding yet more fuel to the fire that burned in her core, his hands cupped and caressed, abandoned and then quickly returned to her breasts in eager demanding movements.

Seeking his mouth, she turned her head. Their lips met hungrily, expressing their need, their passion, their love. Slowly his right hand left her breast and traveled again to the resilient flesh of her belly, moving lower and lower until it encountered the wide elastic band of her bikini pants. His fingers pressed against her creamy skin and effortlessly slipped under the flimsy barrier. As his hand moved lower Danielle's mental sensibilities disappeared, and she became a sensorial creature. Her world became Steve—his touch, his sound, his scent, the marvelous anguish he created with his hands.

As he moved lower and then lower still, she felt herself teetering on a precipice. When, with consummate loving and tenderness, his hand went past the triangular mound of softly curling hair to touch the exquisitely sensitive core of her sensual being—probing, caressing, stroking, making her awareness disappear in an explosive burst of aching need—she cried out his name. "Steve!" It was a question, a statement, a plea, a demand. Instinctively, unconsciously, her hips began to move with the rhythm of his touch.

Because he had been making love to her with his eyes, with his words, since that first day, it took only the gentlest urgings before she began to feel the unmistakable stirrings of the climactic journey he would have her take. But it was a journey she did not want to take alone.

"Steve," she gasped. "You must stop—"

He held her closer. "Don't fight it, Danny. Just let go. Let me do this for you."

"Not without—" she cried, but there was no turning back. She felt the swell of incredible pleasure; waves of delectation swept her higher and higher until she reached a breathtaking peak . . . and then the pulsating release.

Danielle gasped. She leaned heavily against Steve, the back of her head resting on his shoulder. When her breathing had returned to normal she said, "You've given me such beauty, Steve. But it held no satiation or contentment. I want you every bit as much now as I did before." She turned her face to meet his seeking mouth. Her body twisted. The curving swell of her hip pressed into the heat and hardness of his desire.

He lifted her. Her arms wrapped around his neck. "As I recall, the lady requested a bed," he said.

"Right now," she answered, "the lady would make love to the gentleman in the middle of the Sahara Desert."

"In all that sand?" His deep need to make love to her shone through despite the lightness of his words. "Are you trying to tell me something?"

"If you'd do something beside stand here," she chided, "I wouldn't have to try to tell you, I could show you."

"There's only one minor problem. . . ."

"And that is?"

"I have no idea where the bedroom is."

Danielle glanced over his shoulder. "Who cares about a bedroom? There's a lovely sofa over there...." She ran her hand up the back of his neck, grasped his hair and brought his head down, meeting his mouth with her own. Her tongue lingered on his lips, teasing the silky outside before exploring the warm interior. "If the sofa seems too far, the carpet right here is as thick and as soft as a lambskin rug."

If a heart could indeed sing, Steve was sure a truer sweeter melody had never been sung than the one he felt inside him now. Joy? Ecstasy? Euphoria? There were no words. How would a man dying of thirst describe a drink of water? Or a man long lost at sea describe the sighting of land? Only now that she had come back into his life did he realize just how terribly lonely he had been.

Without effort, without even knowing she was doing so, Danny had exposed and made vulnerable again the inner man he had kept hidden since leaving Nevada years before. In the process she had opened old wounds he had thought healed and had made him susceptible to new ones. But it was a trade he had gladly made. To know her love again, he would risk anything—everything.

He caught her lower lip between his own, deepened the kiss, then raised his head. "We are going to start out our new life together in a bedroom on a bed." A roguish smile lit his eyes. "We can experiment with the other rooms and other furniture later."

"We'll never have time for anywhere else if we don't get started," she prompted.

"Are you going to be like this in our old age?"

"Probably worse."

"Hot damn. . . ." His voice was a sensual rasp. "I knew clean living would pay off someday."

Using equal amounts of intuition and assumption, Steve headed in the direction he guessed would produce the bedroom. He strode down a long hallway, turning only once before coming to a room with massive double doors. Danielle reached down, turned the knob and pushed against the oak door. An involuntary cry came from her throat when she saw the room, the same size, luxury and view as the one they had just left. She glanced at Steve and swallowed. "Pretty, isn't it?"

His laugh was warm and spontaneous. "It's not bad if you like this sort of thing."

She looked again at the four-poster bed, larger than any she had ever seen, at matching chairs covered in raw silk that sat in front of the fireplace, at the cherrywood dresser. "I think, if I try real hard, all this just might start to grow on me after a while."

"I love you, Danny," he said softly.

Her gaze returned to his face. Gone was the earlier playfulness. In its place was a look that bypassed her mind and spoke directly to her soul. Somehow, in the years they had been apart, their love had continued to be nurtured and had grown. Where their hearts came together there existed no vacuum, no time of separation. They were, they always had been, bound to each other, incapable of sharing with anyone else the love that had been destined for them alone.

"I would have waited for you forever," she said.

Steve walked to the bed and tenderly placed her on the thick quilted spread. Bending, he pressed a kiss to her stomach before pulling down the brief nylon pants she wore. When he had slipped them from her feet he retraced the path to her hips, trailing his fingers along the softness of her inner thighs. Quickly he stepped free from the last of his own clothing, and then the mattress yielded to his weight and he was beside her.

He enfolded her, holding her against the length of him. He moved as if to cover her with his own body, but instead continued the lithe graceful roll and pulled her on top of him. Cradling her head between his hands he brought her mouth to his. The kiss was a demand, a surrender.

"Will the day come when you tire of hearing me tell you that I love you, Danny?"

"Could I tire of my sustenance?" She pressed her mouth to his chin, to the base of his throat, working free of his hold as she moved lower, kissing the smooth skin of his chest, stopping her journey only to seek the turgid points in the soft mat of hair. When she found the small mounds of flesh she made moist circles around them with her tongue, then gently captured the centers with her teeth. She felt his quickening heartbeat as she continued moving lower, pressing her lips to the slight concave of his belly.

His stomach tightened, growing taut in anticipation as she moved lower still. Her lips had barely felt the heat of his desire when she heard his groan and felt herself being lifted. "Another time, Danny, my love," he breathed. "Today what I want is to feel myself inside of you. I want that special warmth, the enfolding, the sharing making love with you brings."

He kissed her lightly on the forehead and shifted her so that she lay beside him. "Now, however, what I want to do is to look at you," he said.

Defensively, automatically, she moved to cover herself. He stopped her. "You won't believe me when I tell you how beautiful you are unless I've truly looked at you."

"Not now," she said.

"Why?"

She studied the hair on his chest as if seeking her answer there. "I want to be perfect for you. Right now, in your imagination at least, I am." And to prove her point, "The woman you've dreamed about for the last ten years didn't have a farmer's tan on her arms and throat, or legs so white you couldn't tell where the sheets left off and they began."

Tilting her head so that she had to meet his gaze, he looked deeply into her eyes. "Or a waist quite so small...." His words were loving, his eyes full of wanting. "Your hips are exactly as I remembered. They still curve as gently, as invitingly." His hand left hers. When it reached her hip his palm pressed intimately against the bone, his long fingers splayed over the curve. "It even feels the way I remembered." He reached past the sweeping curve and around to her buttocks. "Now this marvelous piece of anatomy seems slightly fuller—a little more rounded. And incredibly sexy. My hand goes all twitchy every time you walk past."

She smiled. "You should have said so earlier—you know I can't stand to see a man suffer. I'm sure we could have worked something out."

"*Now* you tell me," he sighed. Slowly his hand traced an invisible line up her side, stopping at her shoulder. "I'm not sure about this," he said, pressing his lips to the softly rounded edge. "I've never been able to figure out why, when basically they function the same, your shoulders look so enticing, so ready to be nuzzled, and mine look so ordinary." He followed the natural line from her shoulder inward. "And why," he went on, "what is merely a collarbone on me is such an erotic area on you."

His fingers moved lower. "And this gentle swelling. . . ." Languidly he caressed the creamy beginning of her breast. "How this haunted my dreams. And this. . . ." His hand moved lower still. "Shall I tell you how accurately I remembered your breasts—the touch, the feel, the look—how they swell slightly when you're aroused? Would you like to know," he murmured, his mouth replacing his hand, "what feelings go through me . . . when I take the nipple in my mouth . . . and feel it grow rigid against my tongue?"

"Yes," she breathed. "Tell me . . . show me."

But the time for words had passed. All that remained were the fevered mute messages his mouth relayed as he took first one and then the other aching nipple between his lips, stroking, caressing, gently pulling each further into his mouth.

She ran her hands through his hair, urging him nearer as she arched her back to press herself closer to him still. Her breasts, her thighs, her stomach became infused with the heat of desire. A thin sheen of dampness coated her skin.

Possessively Steve's hand traveled the inside of her legs until his palm came to rest on the golden brown mat of curls. With tender hesitant strokes his fingers penetrated the warm welcoming interior. She felt as though she had been sensitized to feel only his touch. Where her body came in contact with the down bedspread she felt nothing; where a wisp of Steve's hair lay lightly against her arm she felt her nerve endings respond explosively.

"Danny—" he looked at her with a plea, a demand in his eyes "—want me!"

Could he not see that she trembled with her need for him? "Every part of me cries out for your touch. How could I want you more?"

"Want me tomorrow . . ." he whispered huskily, his fears finding voice.

She caught her breath. Despite all she had forsaken to be with him he still harbored apprehension. But then, she realized, perhaps it was because of all she had forsaken. "I will love you, I will want you, for tomorrow—" she brushed a kiss against his lips "—and for all the tomorrows for the rest of our lives."

His hand gently clasped her shoulder and he eased her against the bed. She welcomed him into her body, into her heart, into the very essence of her. Their coming together was a celebration, a commitment, a song of life . . . an unspoken promise of forever.

8

THE NEXT MORNING Danielle discovered Steve no longer ate hearty breakfasts. A cup of coffee and a quick perusal of the morning paper were his usual fare now, he told her. It took a little less than four and a half minutes by the kitchen clock for her to get him to change his mind when the smell of her own bacon and eggs wafted through the house and out the door to the sheltered sun porch. She wasn't the least surprised when she looked up and saw him filling the doorway.

"Back for a refill on the coffee already?" she innocently asked, popping a broken bit of bacon into her mouth.

A slow lopsided smile dimpled Steve's cheek. He looked at the quantity of toast and bacon on the counter and the four eggs in the large frying pan. "Quite an appetite you have this morning."

She turned back to the stove to hide her answering smile. "You know how it is with us country folks; when we work hard, we eat hearty."

"Work?" he asked, coming up to stand behind her. He put his arms around her waist, his cheek resting against her temple. "I don't remember any *work*." His hands moved higher to brush against the underside of her breasts.

"You know how it is, one man's work...." His thumbs moved in short enticing strokes, and she went on, "Keep that up and your eggs will be Frisbees."

"Man cannot live on eggs alone."

"Maybe not." She felt herself losing ground. "But this *woman* would at least like them to be a part of her diet."

His tongue lightly stroked her ear. "Did I hear you say 'my' eggs would be Frisbees?"

"You didn't really think I was going to eat all this by myself, did you?"

He abruptly released her. "Oh, well, then. Don't let me disturb you."

She whirled around, wielding the spatula like a weapon. "Oh, so now the truth comes out."

He broke off a piece of bacon, looked up and winked. "Everything in its proper order."

But somehow between the cooking and the serving, the proper order became rearranged when, overly warm in her heavy chenille robe, Danielle started to remove the garment and Steve insisted on helping. They later discarded the breakfast Danielle had cooked and started anew.

THEY SPENT the afternoon gathering shells and exploring the grounds. When the early evening shadows had grown long and encompassing, Steve announced it was time to prepare for their dinner in

Carmel. He claimed the shower first, saying he had twice the body to wash salt water and sand from and therefore had preemptive rights. He was only a little surprised but a lot delighted when moments later Danny joined him in the large tile enclosure. Snuggling close, she cunningly commandeered the largest portion of the water. After several stretching maneuvers and artful moves with her hip she nudged him out of the spray entirely.

"Boy, salt water sure makes you feel sticky," she said, washing the day's accumulation from her arms.

Patiently Steve stepped to the other side to catch the overlapping spray. "Just another of its many charms," he answered.

Purposely Danielle shifted slightly so that she again blocked the water. "I think I could really grow to like this place," she went on conversationally. "I bet it's really something when there's a storm."

Steve stepped back and leaned against the cool tile, crossing his arms. He considered his options. In a tone that matched hers, he said, "I understand a couple of years ago the storms were so bad around here that they washed all the sand from the beaches—along with several homes." Surreptitiously his hand reached for the control to the second shower head directly behind the one Danielle was using.

"How terrible." She had started to turn to face him when the blast of cold water from the second shower head struck. Gasping in surprise she backed into the corner. Fire lit her eyes when Steve calmly touched finger to tongue and made two imaginary lines in the air.

"You realize what this means, don't you?" she said. "It's all out war!" A shiver raised goose bumps on her arms.

He turned the control back to off and reached for her. "Come here," he demanded gruffly. Enfolding her in his arms, he briskly rubbed her back and derrière. "Let's pretend we've had the war and discuss the peace treaty."

The water made their bodies wonderfully slick and somehow more pliant. The feel of her softness against his rigid planes—her breasts yielding to his chest, her stomach yielding to his male hardness—had become more pronounced, more intense.

His lips tasted slightly salty, his shoulder sweet. His hands moved with unrestricted freedom cupping her buttocks, stroking her legs, gently kneading her stomach.

This time the loss of awareness to her surroundings became an actual sensation Danielle could follow. First came the quickening of her heart, followed by the acute, radiating warmth from the pit of her midsection. Then came the hunger, the need, and the disappearance of all else.

Swept away in the same overwhelming flood of yearning that gripped Danielle, Steve reached down and grasped her knee, bringing it up to ride against his hip. She caught her breath before a little cry of surprise escaped her lips as he carefully penetrated, then moved inside of her. It was awkward, it was restricted; it was achingly, breathtakingly beautiful.

When at last their passions were spent, Danielle leaned against Steve like a rag doll. Slowly she again became aware enough to feel the light spray of water on the backs of her calfs. Wearing a contented smile she looked up into his passion-sated eyes. "We simply have to stop meeting like this."

He kissed the end of her nose. "Never."

She entwined her fingers in the tightly curling hair on his chest. "I suppose you'd have us doing this kind of thing when we're eighty."

He covered her wandering hand with his own. "If we don't have a problem at seventy-nine, why should eighty bother us?"

The future seemed so promising.

THE SUN HAD BECOME a rapidly disappearing orange globe casting its final farewell to a gaudily colored sky by the time they were finally out of the shower. Steve stood at the bedroom window watching the day's last hurrah as he ran a towel over his damp hair. Coming out of the bathroom, Danielle watched him a moment, filled with a throat-tightening love. Quietly she crossed the room, slipped her arms around his waist and laid her cheek against his broad back. "Let's not go out tonight," she suggested. "The kitchen is full of food."

"Want me all to yourself?" He laid his arms over hers. She hesitated a moment before answering, finally settling on something halfway between the truth and the light, easy reply that had first come to mind. "If I could, I would have us stay like this forever."

She felt him suddenly grow tense. "Are your doubts about coming to New York growing, Danny?" he prodded.

"No," she lied too quickly.

Not knowing the words to use to destroy her doubts, he let her have her lie.

They ate their dinner picnic style in the bedroom on the floor in front of the fireplace. Steve sat opposite Danielle, sharing his food with her as naturally and as easily as he shared everything else. She had started to tell him that if she continued to eat her food and half of his, she wouldn't be able to get through the door of his airplane for the flight to New York. Instead she simply eased her meal of assorted cheeses, crackers, sliced cold meat and fruit onto his plate and enjoyed the peculiarly exciting and sensual pleasure of having her food placed in her mouth by him.

In a quiet moment she watched the firelight play on his deeply tanned legs, chest and arms. "How do you stay so dark when you work inside all the time?" she wondered aloud.

"It's the firelight—and the fine sheen of sweat I seem to be sporting," he teased. "I'm not really this dark."

She refused to acknowledge the gentle barb over her insistence on a fire on a lovely summer evening. "It's more than that," she insisted. "You're almost as dark as you ever were." Had it not been for the uneven lighting, she would have sworn she saw him flush uncomfortably. "Well?" she prodded.

He brushed the hair from his forehead. "I use the sunlamps at the club where I work out," he finally said in a rush.

At first she didn't understand. Then her eyes widened in disbelief. "You mean you actually spend time under a light bulb to get a tan? Don't you ever get out to enjoy the real thing?"

"Not as much as I should."

"How much?"

"Hardly ever."

"Well, what *do* you do with your time off?"

"I go out." It was obvious he was struggling with the answer. "There's usually one or two social functions I attend every week."

"With friends?"

"Yes, sometimes. Mostly, though, it's on business," he admitted. He caught the flash of unease in her eyes despite her attempt to hide it from him. *Dammit!* a frustrated voice echoed through him. Their marriage would never work if she hid her feelings from him.

He reached for her hand. "Danny, look at me." And when she did he continued, "After I finally acknowledged that no one would ever come into my life who could take the place you had carved in my heart I had to find a way to fill the emptiness. My work became my life. If you will just understand that, you will understand the man I've become." He looked down to where his thumb rubbed lightly across the back of her hand. "Another thing you should try to understand—many things are different in a city like New York."

"I know—"

"More different than you realize or can even imagine right now." His look begged her to try to understand. "Believe it or not, in New York it's perfectly acceptable practice to get your tan from a light bulb."

"It just seems so . . . so—"

"So unmanly?" he queried.

For him to speak her thoughts aloud made her realize how foolish they were. She tried to return his smile. "It seems you need only scratch one small-town lady and you come up with one small-minded prejudice."

"Don't be so hard on yourself." He tugged on her hand and she came to him. His lips, his touch, the magical things he did to her with only a softly spoken word of love made her forget about tans and New York and. . . .

A FULL MOON reflecting off the ocean filled the bedroom with a blue-white light. Danielle had no trouble telling where she was, but she did wonder what had awakened her. And then she heard a poignant cry and immediately knew it was the same sound that had dragged her from the depths of sleep.

"Steve," she called out sleepily. "Are you all right?" When there was no answer she waited a moment, dis-

carding the last remnants of sleep, trying to decide if
the sound had been real or a part of her dream. She
turned to Steve, propping herself up on one arm and
reaching out for his shoulder with the other. The
heartbreaking cry filled the room again.

"Ste—" she choked, the rest of his name dying in her
throat, her hand hanging suspended in midair. The
cry bespoke such complete anguish that Danielle was
forced to share the unknown pain. Still she did not
touch him, afraid to intrude on the private hell that
made his shoulders shudder with silent sobs.

Was he dreaming? If only she could see his face.
And then the cry again tore the silence and she hesitated no longer. Slipping from beneath the covers, she
ran to the other side of the bed and knelt down beside
him.

"Steve—" She caught her breath when she saw his
face. Never had she seen such torment, such suffering. Her hand went to his cheek; she found it damp.
"Steve!" she cried, her alarm increasing to the point
of panic.

Slowly his expression changed as he fought to leave
the depths of sleep. He opened his eyes and immediately knew what had happened. He could hide from
her no longer. He closed his eyes again in a sigh, then
opened them in resignation. "I'm sorry if I scared
you," he said softly.

"Are you all right?"

"Yes. . . ." He shifted, making room for her to crawl
into the bed beside him. "It's just a dream I have oc-

casionally." Perhaps this would be the last time and there would be no need to tell her.

She joined him on the bed, fitting herself into his side, her head on his shoulder, her arm flung possessively across his chest. "That was not 'just a dream,'" she said.

How he wished he could tell her. But to tell her of his nightmare was to give her one of her own. "Danny, please understand . . . I can't tell you about this."

"Why?" Were there to be secrets between them, then?

He knew by the way she asked that she would be hurt no matter what he did. He struggled for words that would hurt the least. "This is an old dream. One I had every night when I first came back from Vietnam. It finally stopped a few years ago. It must have returned because of all that's happened these last two weeks." His grip tightened slightly on her shoulder as if to emphasize his next words. "It has nothing to do with you."

"If seeing me again can make the dream come back, it does have something to do with me," she insisted.

"The dream itself has nothing to do with you, or nothing to do with us."

"Then why won't you tell me what it is?"

"I. . . ." If only he could. "I can't."

"Why?"

She felt him slowly release his breath. "Because it would hurt you," he said, his words spoken barely above a whisper.

"You're trying to protect me from knowing how Frank died," she answered as softly.

Her words were like the edge of a razor, cutting his arguments and defenses from him with a quick clean stroke.

"How did you know?" he finally asked.

"I've always known you didn't tell any of us the whole truth. What I didn't know was how you suffered by keeping it to yourself. Maybe you were right to say nothing then, but you're not now."

He wiped his hand across his forehead. Now that he had been handed the key to unlock the Pandora's box of horrors he had carried around for so long, he couldn't bring himself to use it. "It was such a long time ago. Maybe it would be better left alone."

"Ten minutes is not such a long time ago. To suffer the way you were. . . ."

"Danny, you couldn't begin to understand what it was like over there." He sighed. "You shouldn't have to."

"I will never understand any of it if you don't tell me." As she waited for him to wage his internal battle, she listened to the steady ceaseless rhythm of the ocean caressing the shore and thought of the tragedy they had already shared.

"Going to Vietnam seemed like . . . like we were not only on the other side of the world, but that it had been turned upside down too. Death became as casual, as ordinary as commercials on television. Children not only died, Danny—they killed." Again he paused. "I remember once half the men in our platoon died fighting for one lousy hill; and then it seemed like the minute it was ours, we packed up and left.

"Frank and I got to the point that we clung to each other like two sane men in a madhouse. Toward the end, even though the old-timers told us it was bad luck to do so, we started counting the days until we would be going home. We had sixty-two days left—two crummy thirty-one day months."

Danielle waited for him to go on, suddenly knowing he had been right—she didn't want to hear what he would tell her.

"We were on a reconnaissance mission—it was a pretty morning, real quiet. Too quiet. I saw Frank go down the same time I heard the first shots. He must have walked right into them. There was a field between us so it took me a minute or so to get to him...."

Danielle opened her eyes wide, concentrating on the dim image of the flowered wallpaper opposite her, fighting the mental images his words created.

"I pulled him into a sheltered area . . . out of the line of fire. He was hurt—" Steve held his breath, not wanting to go on, unable to stop. Slowly his breath escaped in a poignant sigh. "He was hurt pretty bad...bad enough that there wasn't much pain. Later, we talked about that. He asked me to tell him about the wounds and how they might affect him when he got home. I lied." Again he rubbed his forehead.

"The battle was over within minutes. It was just another one of those hit-and-run kind of things that happened all the time over there. Only this time our captain decided he wanted to go after them. Before he left he called in the helicopters for Frank. For two days they tried to land; the sniper fire was just too heavy. Frank and I figured the platoon had been led on some wild-goose chase and that he was being used as bait to lure the chopper within shooting distance. Each time it tried to come in, they let it get a little closer before opening fire.

"I've never believed it would have made any difference for Frank if he could have been picked up that first day. But even hurt as bad as he was, it took him a long time to die. Not until the third day was I absolutely sure he was gone.

"We talked for the first two days . . . about all kinds of things. I remember him saying that you had a terrible crush on me. I told him you were just a kid and that you'd get over it. At the end of the first day he stopped moving his legs. By the middle of the second day, it was his hands."

Steve breathed a long, shuddering sigh. "Ground troops arrived the third day and helped to get the chopper in. Even though he was already dead, they let me go with him. The rest you know . . ."

A tear slid across her nose to fall softly against his chest. "And when you came home it was to watch your father die, a day at a time. How it must have hurt to stay as long as you did after your father was gone. I wish I had known."

"I wanted to protect you." His hand stroked her hair. "I think I also must have felt that if I had to use Frank's and my father's deaths to get you to come with me, you didn't love me as much as you said you did." He kissed the place he had stroked. "My God, saying it aloud makes it sound so stupid."

She couldn't answer him. There was a tightness in her throat and chest that made words impossible. How could she not have known how he suffered? Why hadn't she understood what had driven him from Star Valley? She need only summon the memory of his pleading with her to go with him and it was as clear and sharp as if it had happened that morning. How could she had been so blind?

With a heart wrenching sob she turned to him, burying her face against his chest. "I'm . . . so sorry," she cried. "I should . . . I should have known."

He held her, feeling a strange mixture of sorrow for the pain he had caused, and relief to have finally shared the nightmare that had haunted him for so long. "There was no way you could have known," he answered.

"I knew how close you and Frank were—I knew how much you loved your father and how alone you were when they both died. I should have understood how you felt, what you went through."

"Danny, stop it." He gently forced her chin up so that she had to look at him. "You were young. You had the loss of Frank to deal with too. Your world had turned upside down as much as mine when your parents started laying the responsibility of the ranch on your shoulders."

No matter what she said, no matter how true the statement, she knew he would not let her take the blame for what had happened between them ten years ago. "I love you so very, very much," she said. "I'm so sorry for what happened, for what I—"

"I know," he whispered, stopping her from going further. "It's your love that has made my life special again. I've known a joy these last two weeks I haven't known since we separated. I'd almost forgotten how good life can really be."

For the rest of the night they held each other in a newfound intimacy. When they welcomed the morning, it was with a love made stronger through a sorrow finally shared.

9

STEVE QUIETLY REACHED for Danielle's hand as the Learjet started to land at La Guardia Airport. She reciprocated with a gentle squeeze and tentative smile.

"Imagine a grown woman letting a city intimidate her," she said.

"You wouldn't be the first."

"I keep telling myself it's only Reno all grown up."

Steve smiled. "Just remember when anything gets this big it's bound to have had a few growing pains."

She wrapped her fingers around his hand. "I can't shake the feeling that I'm a country bumpkin on her first 'gee whiz' trip to the big city." She didn't add that the "country bumpkin" had been perfectly contented to stay in the country forever.

Their jet bumped lightly down on the long asphalt runway. When they were taxiing in, Steve unbuckled her seat belt, then turned his attention to peeling her fingers from his hand. She grinned sheepishly in acknowledgment of her iron grip. "Want to arm wrestle?"

"Breathe deeply!" he commanded.

She complied, then asked, "What is that supposed to do for me?"

"If I can get you to do it often enough, you'll pass out. With any luck you won't come to before we reach the apartment."

She glared at him. "Funny, Maddox. Real funny."

They were met by one of the company limousines, fully outfitted with a bar, television, telephone and miniature wedding cake. Steve wrote himself a mental memo to personally thank the crew responsible for the special smile of pleasure on Danielle's face that the cake brought—a smile that didn't fade even in the heart of the city.

They took a circuitous route, traveling on streets and past landmarks that, even to Danielle, sounded familiar. Broadway, Time Square, Fifth Avenue and finally, Park Avenue . . . names anyone who had read a book or newspaper or had seen a movie or watched a television show about New York knew as well as the streets in their own home towns.

At stoplights Danielle would select one of the pedestrians and play a childhood game of guessing who they were, what they did and why they were standing on that particular corner at that very moment in time. She was amazed and delighted at the widely different answers Steve gave, some terribly romantic, others pragmatic. Deep down they both knew, but neither acknowledged, that her game had very serious undertones. It was a way for someone who came from a town where she knew everyone, to personalize a city that had literally millions of people walking its streets.

As they neared Steve's apartment a young woman stepped from the curb at the corner. Danielle uttered a strangled cry, certain they would hit her. Never slowing, the driver of their car missed her by inches. Danielle swung around to see the woman, totally unconcerned, cross the street against the light.

"Did you see that?" She looked at Steve to see that he was staring at her with an amused look in his eyes.

"Sometimes New Yorkers watch the traffic as well as the lights. If there's an opening, they cross." He shrugged at her wide-eyed expression. "Amazingly, it works. I know people who swear the whole city would come to a stop if everyone waited for a green light before they crossed the street."

"Is that why there are so many horns honking?"

"Those are mostly taxis'. Frankly," he bent closer as if sharing a secret, "I think they've worked out a coded communication system between themselves, but I haven't been able to prove anything yet."

"Is it like this all the time?" she asked, ignoring his playfulness.

He shook his head. "The trucks take over in the early morning. Without them Manhattan would perish. It is totally dependent on the outside for everything."

She groaned. "Quick, tell me something good."

He laughed and pulled her into the shelter of his arm. "First and foremost, I'm here. That should count for something, shouldn't it?"

"Unfair, Maddox, we're talking about the city, not you."

"Well, let me see. I suppose those who live in Washington, D.C., would be quick to argue the point, but I happen to believe this little section of earth is the hub of the civilized world. Even if you forget that this is the headquarters of the United Nations, the museums and theater are among the best anywhere. There's an excitement here . . . an energy level I've never felt anywhere else." His enthusiastic discourse reminded Danielle of Ben a month after he'd stopped smoking.

"Did this feeling just kind of grow on you after you had been here awhile?" she asked, her voice filled with hope.

"It was something I felt the first day."

"Then I have a few hours yet. . . ." She snuggled closer as if subconsciously seeking reassurance.

"I'm not worried," he said. "This place has converted millions before you."

Just then the telephone buzzed. Danielle fought the silly smile she felt hovering at the idea of receiving a call in a moving car. Somehow a telephone in a limousine seemed ostentatious, while the CBs they used for communication on the ranch seemed only practical.

Steve answered, listened, then made a few terse comments before replacing the receiver.

Danielle waited expectantly. "Well?" she finally prodded.

It was as if he had become mentally immersed in another world and was no longer aware of her sitting beside him. He looked at her with troubled eyes. "Huh?" he asked, as much in reaction to the expression on her face as her query.

"The phone call?"

He took her hand in his. "You'll have to be patient with me. It's going to take a while to realize there's someone beside me who might be interested in what I do."

"And that is...."

"What? Oh, the telephone call. Rydal Electronics is balking at giving us full control over their employees. Elaine has set up a phone conference with them for four o'clock this afternoon." His fingers tapped thoughtfully against the seat. When he noticed that she looked as if she expected him to go on, he said, "Rydal is a medium-sized, family-owned, computer company in Texas."

"And Elaine is...."

"Elaine Carson—she was chosen to head the team we're getting ready to send to Rydal's." His voice grew harsh. "But if Marvin Rydal keeps going the way he has been, he'll find himself fighting off the creditors all alone."

"I take it you're not crazy about the guy?"

"He inherited the company three years ago. Since then he's damn near run it dry to support himself in the style he felt was owed to him. He's not so stupid that he doesn't realize the profit on the sale of a healthy company is far greater than on one about to go under. He considers us a necessary nuisance, nothing more, probably a whole lot less."

"What will you tell him?"

"To sign the papers the way they are or get someone else to do the work."

"Is there anyone else?"

"Not many, but there are a few."

The car stopped in front of a tall, gray block-stone building, its facade covered in a film of black soot similar to many other buildings Danielle had noticed on their journey through the city. She glanced across the street at the park. At least there was some relief here from the monochromatic gray she had seen everywhere else. She tried to smile. "Is that the famous Central Park over there?"

Nodding, Steve returned her smile. "That's it. And this," he indicated the building she had already noticed, "is home."

Danielle swung around again to look out the opposite window. A lump formed in her throat as she peered past the pedestrians to get a closer look at her new home. "So this is where you live?" She forced a lightness into her voice.

Steve wasn't fooled. "It's a little more inviting on the inside," he said, unable to keep a smile from his face as he thought how impressed a native New Yorker would have been at the prime location and how completely unimpressed Danny obviously was.

"I didn't mean—" The car door swung open. When the chauffeur held out his hand to help her, Danielle's automatic response was to exit from the car rather than make him wait while she continued her discussion.

Steve slid across the seat and called to her. "Here, you'll need this." In his hand was a key. "The apartment is on the top floor. Once you get off the elevator, go to your left. There are only two doors, ours is the first. I'll be home as soon as I can."

"You're not coming with me?" she asked in surprise.

"I'm sorry, Danny. I thought you understood that I would be going to the office for the conference call." He shrugged helplessly. "It's already three-thirty."

"Oh . . . I guess I just didn't think."

As if only then realizing what effect his actions might have on her, Steve reached out to her. "I'm sorry . . ." he said softly.

"It's all right." And when he failed to respond, "Really." She forced a smile. "I'm a big girl now. I think I can find my way from the curb to the top floor of the building."

"I'll come as soon as I can."

Danielle stood beside the doorman and watched Steve's car pull back into traffic. She waved as the limousine merged, a sleek black fish in a sea of yellow taxis, not knowing whether Steve could see her from behind the one-way privacy windows or not, only knowing she suddenly felt terribly alone. She turned to the tall angular man dressed in a maroon military-style uniform who stood beside her. He responded to her tentative smile with one of his own. "You'll be staying with Mr. Maddox?"

"Yes. We were...I'm...." She showed him her hand.

"Congratulations," he said, his voice filled with genuine warmth, his stately manner proper yet welcoming. Already she liked him.

"Thank you, Mr.—"

"Arnold, just Arnold. Been that way for too many years to start using anything else." The brass buttons on his coat sparkled in the late afternoon sun, and his softly curling white hair brushed lightly against his cap. "I'm here to help you in any way I can, so you be sure to call on me if I can be of service."

"Is right now too soon?" She shrugged expressively. "I don't know where to find the elevators."

He gave her a tiny elegant bow, a twinkle in his soft brown eyes. "Certainly one of my easiest requests. If you'll follow me?"

With Steve's simple instructions precisely repeated by Arnold, Danielle had no trouble finding the apartment. She stood in front of the cream-colored door for a long time, unable to go inside. Old familiar fears had returned to haunt her as easily as the key slid into the lock. In the solitude of the small hallway she momentarily gave in to her feelings. Her shoulders slumped wearily as she closed her eyes and leaned her head against the door. *Stop it!* her mind demanded of her wayward emotions. *It doesn't make any difference that he's not with you.*

But it did!

Somewhere beyond the door a telephone rang. Its summons sounded distant, beckoning, insistent. Without further thought Danielle turned the door handle and entered the apartment. It took a moment and some confused searching for her to realize the familiar sound came from a gracefully curved piece of white plastic that sat on an end table near a lamp.

"Hello?" she said, the lone word more a question than a greeting.

"Welcome home," Steve answered. And then, his voice a deep caress, "I'm sorry I'm not there with you, Danny."

"I hardly noticed." She fought the spasms in her throat.

"Liar...."

"You think you know me pretty well, don't you?" Again she forced a lightness she didn't feel into her voice.

He ignored her attempt at easy banter. "It was stupid and insensitive of me to drop you off like that. I should have had you come to the office with me so that we could at least be together when you entered your new home. You have every right to be angry... and hurt."

"Steve—it's all right! Would you please stop thinking of me as though I were some fragile china doll?"

"Not a doll . . . more like a precious piece of porcelain."

She blinked back the tears that had suddenly appeared in her eyes. "Oh, is that right?" How normal she sounded. "That means you think of me as flat, smooth and cold, I suppose. Boy, I can see I've got some work ahead of me."

There was a pause. Danny could hear horns honking in the background and knew he was still in the car.

"Danny," he said softly. "I know what you're doing...I love you for it. I love you more than you'll ever know."

"Hurry home," she whispered.

"I'll be there as soon as I can."

Slowly Danielle placed the receiver back in its freeform cradle, reluctant to let go of even the most tenuous contact. She let her purse strap slip from her shoulder, dropping the brown leather bag beside the telephone, then reached up to wipe the lingering moisture from her eyes. She looked around her. She had seen rooms like this in magazines—magazines in doctors' and dentists' offices, never the kind subscribed to by the ranch. Decorated in glass and chrome and expensive man-made fabrics with everything forming stark clean lines, it was a glowing tribute to the twentieth century. Even the images depicted in the paintings had been created with as few bold brush strokes as needed to convey their somewhat obtuse meanings.

And except for two of the paintings, it was all in black and white. Everything from the snowy-white depths of the lush carpeting to the midnight-black drapes at the wall of windows.

The idea of using black and white as decorator colors was as alien to her as the style of furniture. In the dust and wind of the Nevada desert, there was no such thing as pure white, only beige. Every particle of dust on shiny furniture became showcased. Danielle looked at the tabletops in the room—they reflected only pure, untouched splendor. It was as if the room were in a vacuum where nothing from the real world, the world she had known before, existed or penetrated.

Forcefully she fought the feelings of unease that bordered uncomfortably on panic. She would adjust, she mentally insisted. In time she would adjust. All she needed in order to fit into her new life was a little time. She would keep herself busy and eventually she would adapt. That would be the key—keep busy.

Without a backward glance Danielle left the living room and headed in the direction she assumed the kitchen would be. The ultramodern, spacious and spotless room was behind a wide sliding door on the other side of the narrow dining area. Preparing a dinner from the odds and ends she found in the cupboards, freezer and refrigerator would be a challenge. Just the thing to keep her occupied until Steve arrived.

THE CASSEROLE Danielle created was dried out and shrunken by the time Steve arrived at nine-thirty. Standing at the living-room window watching the lights of the traffic far below, she was startled when he suddenly, noiselessly, appeared beside her. "I didn't hear you come in," she said, tilting her head to accept his kiss.

"You looked a thousand miles away." He put his arms around her waist. "Or was it more like three thousand?" he asked intuitively.

To deny the obvious would be foolish. "The contrast is so—" she struggled for the word "—so total."

"I forget sometimes."

She laid her head against his shoulder. "Why would you even think about Nevada after all this time?"

"Because of you," he said softly. "No other reason. . . just you."

She knew if she didn't get their conversation on safer grounds, she was liable to give into a sudden, overwhelming impulse to cry. "How did the phone call go?" she asked.

"Rydal wound up giving a hell of a lot more than he wanted to, so in the end we gave a little to make it easier on him. It looks like we'll be going down there next week to get things started." His arms tightened their hold; his lips brushed her temple. "I've just spent the last five hours on Rydal; let's talk about something else. I don't ever want to be one of those husbands who can't leave their work at the office."

"But I'm interested in what you do—"

"Later," he insisted. "For now, let's discuss the delicious smell that greeted me when I came in."

She couldn't help the feeling that a door had somehow closed between them. But she let the subject go, promising herself she would come back to it later. "What would you like to know about that smell?" she bantered. "What it started out like? What it looked like when it was ready to eat? Or maybe what it looks like now?"

"Are you trying to tell me it's caviar and crackers again tonight?"

"I used the crackers in the casserole."

"Mmmm . . . better yet."

"Not a chance. You're also out of caviar."

"Damn."

"However there is some chipped beef in the cupboard."

"Somehow it wouldn't be the same."

"You'll never know. . . ."

"There is no substitute for the real thing."

"You sound like an ad for the dairy council."

"And here I was striving to be a spokesman for the decadent rich."

"They don't need a spokesman. Their life-styles do it for them."

"Meaning?" His lips had moved to the hollow beneath her ear.

"At least a quarter of the cars I've seen pass by in front of this building have been limousines. Where is the common man in this city?"

"Frequently inside the limousines. Most of them are rented by the hour by very ordinary people. In New York limousines are little more than oversize taxis."

"I can't believe your average, common person uses a limousine for daily transportation—even in this city."

"Define common."

"Someone who earns a middle income—secretaries, bookkeepers, clerks—that kind of person."

"The greatest percentage of New Yorkers use the subways, buses or cabs—or if where they're going is within a ten block radius, they walk. Public transportation is really very good here. It has to be. The city would stop dead if everyone owned his own car as people do in Nevada."

She thought a minute. Almost to herself she said, "Then all I need is a map and a bus schedule and I'm ready to go out and conquer—"

Steve laughed. "Hold on a minute. If you want to go somewhere, let me know and I'll arrange for a car to take you."

A puzzled frown creased her forehead. "You can't possibly mean you want me to call you every time I want to go to the store?"

"Either myself or my secretary. Rachel can make the arrangements if I'm not available."

Again she thought for a moment. "And if all I want to do is walk to a store that's just around the block?" Her question was meant to tease; his answer took her by complete surprise.

"I don't want you walking anywhere until we've had a chance to go over a few things."

She studied his face. "You're not kidding, are you?"

"No, I'm not. I don't want you out wandering the streets until you've learned a few of the basics. New York isn't Reno all grown up, Danny," he finally admitted. "This city operates by a different set of rules."

"And those rules are?"

"We'll talk about it later." He touched her lips lightly with his own. "A discussion on street crime in the big city was not what I had in mind for your first night in your new home."

Once again an inner voice told her to let it go for now. She responded readily to the suggestive implication in his words. Snuggling her hips into his she looked up at him through hooded eyes. Slowly, purposely she licked the taste of him from her lips. "Oh? Just what was it that you did have in mind for my first night in my new home?"

"It's something better shown than told."

"Mmmm . . . sounds promising."

With a quick lithe movement Steve bent and caught her up in his arms. Danielle brushed the hair from his forehead. "Need any help finding the bedroom?" she murmured against his lips.

"Did a little exploring, did you?"

"With great trepidation, I might add. It was a relief to discover you weren't as rich, or at least not as obviously rich, as I had feared."

"And what made you change your mind?"

"This apartment," she went on. "I was afraid it would be some big rambling affair. But it's not. They're nothing alike, of course, but as far as square footage, I don't think this place is much bigger than the ranch house."

The puzzled smile on Steve's face became a mysterious laugh. He laid her on the bed and came down beside her, pulling her into his arms. "Before you go mentioning my frugality to anyone, my love, I think you should know that in New York you have to pay a little extra for a panorama of Central Park."

"Whatever it was you had to pay, it was worth it. The view is spectacular, especially at night."

He held her face cradled between his hands. Tenderly he kissed her eyes, her nose, her mouth. "Oh, my wonderful, Danny. I have an entire world to show you—a world I'll be seeing all over again through your eyes."

She stroked his back in ever-widening circles. "Is that world more beautiful than the one we're in right now?" she asked softly.

"Nothing is more beautiful."

Her hands moved on to his waist. "More exciting?"

"Impossible!"

From his waist she moved lower. "More—"

His demanding kiss told her the time for words was over. Eagerly she acquiesced.

THE SKY WAS STILL a dusty black the next morning when Steve gently woke Danielle to kiss her goodbye. Through sleep-filled eyes she saw that he was dressed and ready to leave. "What time is it?"

"Too early for you to get up. Try to go back to sleep."

"But why—"

"I have a lot of work to catch up on." He ran his finger along the strap of her nightgown. "Seems things just kept coming in while I was away pursuing more important matters."

"When will you be home?"

"Right now I have no idea. I'll give you a call." The kiss he gave her told her how reluctantly he was leaving.

"I forgot to tell you that Elaine invited you to go shopping with her today. You'll need something formal for the cocktail party we're invited to this Friday."

"The same Elaine of the Rydal Electronic account?"

He smiled. "The very same. She told me to tell you that she'll phone around nine."

"Steve...." The words seemed stuck in her throat. "I—I, ah, I haven't...I don't...." She took a deep breath. "I can't pay for a new dress right now. I'm going to transfer my own account to a New York bank as soon as I can," she rushed on. "I hadn't anticipated that I would need money so soon or I would have brought more than I did with me."

He took her hand. "Danny, it isn't unheard of for a husband to buy his wife's clothes."

"I know it sounds silly—"

"Stop right there. We both know that you could afford to buy your own clothes—but it's something I want to do. Let me take care of it, please." He kissed her on the cheek, started to leave, then came back for a long promissory kiss on the mouth. "Buy something extravagant."

"But how—"

"Don't worry. I'll take care of it."

Sitting up in bed, she forced a smile as she watched him leave. When he was gone she reached for her robe. Someday soon they were going to have to have a long discussion about money. She had no intention of living off his largess when she had her own income . . . and not a small amount of pride.

ELAINE CARSON PHONED at precisely nine o'clock. During several minutes of introduction and polite conversation, Danielle learned that she and Steve were not just guests at the upcoming party—which she also learned was being thrown by Steve's office— they were the guests of honor. No wonder Steve had requested she buy something special.

"Is eleven a good time for you?" Elaine asked, finalizing their plans.

"Yes, it's fine," she said, mentally adding that they could have chosen any hour and the answer would have been the same.

Danielle hadn't realized how nervous she was about the meeting until the actual moment arrived. When she discovered that Elaine was a woman not unlike all of the others Danielle had known in her lifetime, she let out a long mental sigh of relief.

The woman sitting opposite her in the company limousine looked only an inch or two over five feet tall, and had short black hair, rimless glasses and a full figure that unabashedly proclaimed she occasionally surrendered a battle or two in the war with calories but had not yet lost the war. She was dressed in a beautiful burnt orange linen suit that made her light brown eyes seem shot with gold.

Before they left the curb, Elaine pulled a piece of paper from her pocket. "Steve has given me a list of stores where he has accounts. He said to tell you that he called them and told them you're coming. You're not to worry about anything."

Embarrassed at having someone else involved in what she considered a personal matter, Danielle started to explain, but Elaine stopped her. "Hey, you don't have to tell me how complicated it can get when you move across country. When I came here from San Francisco, my account number was somehow transposed. The transfer from bank to bank became an incredible mess, and I had to wait almost a month before I got any money at all. If it hadn't been for Steve, I would have had to live on beans and yogurt." She screwed up her face. "Ugh! Can you imagine?"

Danielle laughed. "Thanks for the warning. I'll be sure to check everything twice. If I had known I would need money so soon, I could have brought a draft with me. But getting to the bank was on the bottom of a list of things I had to do before I left."

Suddenly serious, Elaine softly said, "It's tough when you first get here. But if you stick it out, the place kind of grows on you after a while."

"Oh, I hope so." She couldn't help but wonder just how much Steve had told Elaine.

"Don't worry. You'll do okay. You look like a fighter to me."

"Thanks." Danielle smiled. "I need all the encouragement I can get."

The chauffeur stopped across the street from a large fountain. As they left the car Elaine pointed to the building behind the tree-lined plaza filled with tourists. "That's the Plaza Hotel. I've made reservations at the Palm Court restaurant for lunch. I hope that's all right."

Danielle's gaze took in the building she had read about so often as a child. "It's more than all right. It will fulfill a childhood dream."

"So you were a fan of Eloise too."

"I spent a great deal of my childhood with my nose in a book dreaming that I would someday get to see the places I read about. I've already taken care of John Steinbeck's California, and it only seems fitting that since I'm in New York I take care of Kay Thompson's

Eloise. I can still remember pretending I was the one who had all those adventures at the Plaza."

"Well, wait until you see *this* place." Elaine indicated the building in front of them and took Danielle's arm. "It defies description."

Discreet windows in which merchandise was displayed with an artist's touch flanked the glass doors leading to Bergdorf Goodman's. As they passed through the boutiquelike sections of the store, Danielle murmured softly to herself, "I'm surprised they don't charge admission to get in."

She was startled to hear Elaine whisper back, "Don't worry, they're making so much on the merchandise they don't have to."

While Elaine pointed out what she considered good and bad buys with the aplomb of a seasoned shopper, Danielle couldn't shake the feeling she really didn't belong in the ultrachic store. Arriving in the formal attire section, Elaine introduced her to a clerk, who immediately whisked her off to a dressing room that was as large as her bedroom had been at the ranch. Within minutes there were a dozen dresses for her to try on, chosen, she assumed, by Elaine. Sequins, satins, silks and beaded sheaths yielded sensuously to her tentative touch. She was amazed. Without asking, Elaine had sent not only the correct size, but Danielle's favorite colors as well.

When the clerk finally realized that Danielle was waiting for her to leave before she tried on any of the

gowns, she exited, saying, "If I can be of any help,
please let me know. I'll be right outside."

"Thank you," Danielle said. After quickly going
through the selection one more time she chose a softly
shirred lemon-yellow gown to try on first. She had to
bite her cheek to keep the silly smile hovering there
from making her appear even more unsophisticated
than she felt. Once she allowed the smile free rein, it
would be impossible to make it go away again, she
knew.

Purposely turning away from the multiple mir-
rors, she studiously avoided catching a glimpse of
herself as she changed, wanting the full effect to be a
surprise. Again the grin hovered. She could remember feeling this way about shopping for a dress only
one other time in her life—for a Grange dance, her
first real date with Steve. As though it were yesterday
she remembered how desperately she had wanted to
look beautiful for him. They were feelings not so different from the ones she had now.

With trembling fingers Danielle pulled the zipper
closed and pressed the tab down. She shut her eyes
and turned: slowly she opened them. For long minutes she stood perfectly still, staring at her reflection.
All that she had been, all that she had left behind,
stared back at her. The beautiful, sensual silk dress
mocked her. Glaringly it told her she did not really
belong there. Unmercifully it screamed that she was
a trespasser in the world she had sought to enter.

Unconsciously her hand went to her throat. Her fingers traced the bronze triangle of flesh, as if by doing so she could blend it with the creamy colored skin beside it. She rubbed her arms, which the long days in the Nevada sun had left so deeply tanned they looked as if they didn't belong to the rest of her body.

Danielle turned from the mirror and looked through the gowns again. There wasn't one she could wear. Slowly, methodically she undressed.

What would she say to Elaine? What could she say? She knew no words to lessen her embarrassment. She sat on a chair in the corner of the dressing room. When fifteen minutes had passed, she left.

Elaine greeted her with an expectant smile. "Well?" she asked.

Danielle rubbed her forehead. It had never been easy for her to lie, no matter how good the reason or how small the lie. "Elaine, I seem to have developed a terrible headache," she said awkwardly. "Would you mind if we did this another time?"

Concern created tiny lines between Elaine's finely arched brows. "Are you sure it's just a headache? You're not coming down with something, are you? Maybe we should call Steve."

"No . . . please don't." The lie became more complicated. "I'm sure it's nothing more than a reaction to all the travel. There's been so much happening lately. . . ."

Elaine studied her closely, a nurse examining a reluctant patient. "Okay. If you're sure."

Twenty minutes later Danielle was back at the apartment. Wearily stepping out of her heels, then bending to pick them up, she was startled to hear a noise in the kitchen. "Steve?" she called. When there was no answer she called again, only louder, "Steve?" Still nothing.

Be reasonable Danielle. Why would a thief be rummaging around in a kitchen?

For toaster...blenders...silver...crystal! an equally forceful inner voice replied.

Holding her shoe so that she could use the heel as a weapon, she crept down the short hallway and into the dining room. The sliding door stood open, letting her maneuver so that she could see inside before she was seen. Danielle stood transfixed. A plump, middle-aged woman with graying hair hummed softly to herself as she put canned goods into the cupboards.

Turning from her chore the woman glanced in Danielle's direction; she let out a high-pitched scream when she spotted her. Clutching her heaving bosom, the woman leaned against the counter. "How did you get in here?" she gasped.

"I have a key." It was the obvious, logical answer.

The woman's eyes narrowed. "Mr. Maddox didn't say nothing about anyone else having a key," she said belligerently.

Danielle squared her shoulders. What next? "He probably hasn't had a chance to tell you yet, but Steve and I were married. I'm Mrs. Maddox."

"Oh, yeah? Since when?"

What had only been simmering reached the boiling point. "Never mind who I am. Who are you?" Danielle demanded, her voice only slightly below a shout.

It was as if she hadn't bothered to ask. "I been working here for over three years now," the woman went on. "No one ever said anything to me about any wife."

Not knowing how else to convince her, Danielle stuck out her hand. "Mr. Maddox and I were married a week ago in Nevada."

"And that rock on your hand is supposed to convince me?"

The merely frustrating had slipped into the ridiculous. "Since you obviously won't listen to me, why don't you call Mr. Maddox?"

"And don't you think I won't." Warily she eased past Danielle on her way to the phone. But it wasn't Steve she called. "Arnold, this is Zelda. There's a woman here claiming she's—" There was a pause. "Is that right?" Another pause. "Well, why the hell doesn't anyone ever tell me anything?" Zelda hung up and turned to Danielle. She looked as conciliatory as a cat with cream on its whiskers. "You can never be too careful around here," she grumbled.

"If that's an apology, I accept," Danielle said, realizing her phantom headache had become real. She pressed her hands against her throbbing temple.

Zelda snorted. "It's about as close as I'll ever come to making one."

"Well, Zelda, perhaps we should start again." The effort at good humor was costing her dearly. "I'm Danielle Hart—" She grimaced. "Danielle *Maddox*." She extended her hand, determined to be friendly to someone Steve had hired, despite her more honest impulse to throw the woman out of the apartment.

"Zelda Kramer." She took Danielle's hand.

"And what exactly is it that you do for Steve?"

"Everything a wife does 'cept sleep with him." She chuckled, obviously enjoying her joke immensely. "Course I don't cook for him too often either but it sounds snappier the other way."

"Do you come in every day?" Danielle fought the sinking feeling in the pit of her stomach. With Zelda around what was left for her to do?

"Three times a week. Monday, Wednesday and Friday."

"You do a beautiful job. The apartment looks more like a showplace—it's incredibly clean."

"Mr. Maddox is real special. Me and him go back a long ways. I always do a little extra for him."

"Well. . . ." Danielle shrugged. She could think of nothing else to say. "I guess I'll leave you to your work." She backed up and ran into the table. "Have you finished the bedroom?"

"Haven't even been in there yet."

"Then I'll take care of it myself later. I'm going in to lie down . . . I have a headache."

"You be sure to tell Mr. Maddox that it was you said not to clean the bedroom. I'm not coming back until Friday, you know."

Danielle tried to smile. "Yes. I guess I'll see you then. . . ." And next Monday and Wednesday and Friday and Monday and. . . .

Carelessly leaving her shoes in the middle of the floor, her purse on the dresser and her jacket on the chair, Danielle wearily dropped onto the bed. She pressed the heels of her hands against her eyes and forced herself to take deep calming breaths. *Time,* she reminded herself. *All she needed was a little more time.* Eventually she would find her niche.

She had never really been that crazy about housework before. Why was it suddenly so important now? Soon they would have children. The children would keep her busy and she would be glad she didn't have housework to do. Clinging to that thought as tenaciously as an astronaut floating outside his spaceship clings to his lifeline, Danielle drifted into unconsciousness.

She was unaware that she had fallen asleep until the doorbell rang and woke her. Jumping out of bed and racing for the door, she made it to the middle of the hallway before a wave of dizziness swept over her. She leaned against the wall and waited for the room to stop spinning. Again the bell chimed. "I'm coming," she called.

"It's Arnold, Mrs. Maddox," a deep voice answered.

Danielle flipped the lock, opened the door and indicated to Arnold that he should come in. "I want to thank you for vouching for me with Zelda," she said, catching her loose hair with her hand and pushing it over her shoulder. "I was afraid for a minute she was going to call the police."

"We've all been a little more cautious than usual since the Websters were robbed last month by a group posing as carpet cleaners."

"Are the Websters in this building?"

"Next door."

"Oh...."

"Don't let it disturb you. It isn't a daily occurrence. Just something to put us all back on our toes." He smiled the same warm smile Danielle had seen the day before. "Now as to why I'm here. This arrived for you." He handed her a silver box with the name "Maxi's," written in bold letters at the bottom.

"For me?" Danielle asked.

"Yes, ma'am. At least that's what the ticket says."

"Thank you," she said absently as she reached for the box.

"My pleasure," Arnold touched the brim of his hat and turned to leave.

"Arnold..." Danielle called out. "I'm not sure how this is done. I don't know...." She let out a big sigh. "Should I give you a tip?"

He laughed. "One of your beautiful smiles is all the tip I ever want from you, Mrs. Maddox."

The smile she gave him in return felt good on her face. "I'm so glad you work here, Arnold."

"Me too, Mrs. Maddox." He tipped his hat and closed the door.

Danielle examined the box, turning it over in her hands, listening to the soft sounds that came from inside. Slowly she walked back to the bedroom, a puzzled frown on her face. She laid the package on the dresser and went over to pick up her shoes. Returning from the closet she sat on the edge of the bed and stared at the silver box. She had only been in New York a little over a day—who would send her a present?

Finally curiosity won out and she went over to the dresser. Gingerly she opened the box. When the top had been set aside she pulled the gummed seal from the crisp white tissue and laid it beside the top. A soft cry of surprise accompanied her quick intake of breath. Lying in the box was a formal gown of shimmering morning yellow. Danielle reached down to touch the dress, lightly running her fingers along the high cowl-like neck.

For long minutes she stood and stared. Then, with trembling hands she withdrew the gleaming gown. A folded piece of paper fluttered to the rug. She reached for it, instantly recognizing Steve's handwriting on the inside.

Saw this in a window on my way to lunch. Knew only a woman with magnificent breasts could carry it off. Immediately thought of you. I'll expect a private showing when I get home.

Love, Steve

Again she looked at the gown, at the high neck and long sleeves and at a back that was bare to the waist. it was the most beautiful, the most sensual garment she had ever seen. The mystery as to who had chosen the gowns at Bergdorf Goodman's, all in the proper size and color, was a mystery no longer.

He knew! Somehow Steve knew what had happened to her earlier that day and had purposely sought and found the dress that would be perfect for her.

Each day she wondered how she could love him more; each day he showed her a way.

10

OUT OF HABIT Steve awoke early Saturday morning. Enjoying a rare moment of inactivity he propped his pillow up behind him and stared at the still-dark bedroom. Forcefully he pushed aside the feelings of guilt that had immediately surfaced when he thought of the office and the work he should be doing there. The team that had been working on the McDowell Textile account for the last nine months was on the verge of losing everything over a group of creditors who refused to grant the company an extension. They would have to find some new way to placate those creditors or it was the end of the line for McDowell and about two hundred of their employees, as well as nine months down the tube for Eagle Enterprises. It would be an unnecessary and tragic loss to everyone concerned. He had never taken losing well, and the idea of losing this company, so close to the turnaround, bothered him even worse than usual.

Danielle stirred in her sleep, turning so that she faced him, snuggling as if seeking his body heat. Unconsciously she reached out, her hand innocently, erotically touching him. Steve smiled. Even in her sleep she was a temptress. He brushed a kiss against her hair.

Would he ever grow used to having her beside him? Would the wonder of it ever wear off? He couldn't shake the feeling that continued to come over him at the most unexpected times, that it was all some cruel, incredibly realistic, dream. It had happened so fast— ten years of such terrible internal loneliness ended in the short space of a month. The script for a movie maybe, not real life.

Sometimes lately with the tumultuous happenings at the office, he would become so deeply immersed in work that he would forget everything else. And then suddenly he would remember. The feelings that came over him then were filled with such warmth, such joy, he honestly felt he knew what it would be like to be hopelessly lost and then found.

The sky was fading to a muted purple as the false dawn gave way to the pervasive, insistent sun. A soft shaft of light fell across Danielle's new dress, lying on the back of a chair opposite the bed. Remembering the party the night before, Steve again smiled.

Although his friends were far too polite and circumspect to say anything, Steve had known Danielle would be exposed to the typical New York attitude toward anything or anyone from west of the New Jersey state line. He knew what they were expecting, what their idea of a woman from the wilds of Nevada would probably look and sound like. But it wasn't what they got. Danielle had not only stunned them with her beauty, she had blatantly charmed them with her eagerness to fall in love with the city they all called home.

Instead of a purse, Danielle had brought an elegant black leather note pad with her to the party, mysteriously answering Steve's queries with, "You'll see." All evening, whenever the moment seemed right, she'd asked the guest who happened to be closest to her to tell her about his or her favorite city, New York. She'd queried them about which sights she should see, which restaurants served authentic cuisine, which plays not to miss. And everything they told her she wrote down in the little black book. Eventually, some time during the evening, everyone she'd met made their way over to Steve to tell him what a charming, brilliant and beautiful wife he had.

After the party, on the way back to the apartment, the gracious role Danielle had adopted was discarded with as little conscience as yesterday's paper. The seam in Steve's pants suddenly developed a compelling fascination as she followed the crisp line up his leg.

"Danielle, if you don't stop that, you're going to make it very difficult for me to get out of this car and blend into a crowd."

"Would you believe," she said, her hand moving higher still, "in all my twenty-nine years, I've never fooled around in a car?"

He caught her hand. "How could you have missed out on one of the great American traditions?"

She gently tugged her hand free. "Seems to me it was because the guy I liked at the time had this thing about sand." Her touch grew bolder. She caught her lip between her teeth to keep from smiling when he gasped in surprise.

"In case you haven't noticed before now, Danny, this limousine is equipped with all the modern features—including a rear-view mirror."

"Don't worry, Maddox. I've taken care of everything. Now stop being such a spoil sport."

Steve glanced forward. The inside mirror had been turned so that it would reflect nothing more than the car's ceiling. "How did you manage—"

"What you don't know, won't hurt you."

By the time they arrived at the apartment fifteen minutes later, Steve was filled with an ache keener than any he had ever felt. The short walk from the car, during which he made Danielle walk in front of him; the seemingly endless elevator ride; the time it took to unlock the door all heightened and honed the growing need inside of him, until he felt like a base piano wire that had been stretched to high C.

As he watched her walk down the hall toward the bedroom he'd mentally pictured her without the seductive garment she wore. In his mind's eye he saw her full breasts, swollen from the same fire that burned through his veins, their dusky nipples rigid with the yearning ache of passion. He saw the dark triangle of hair, he saw....

And then it had become unnecessary for him to imagine any longer. Danielle stood before him, far more beautiful than he could ever conjure in a mere mental image.

Her naked body pressing against him felt like warm sunshine on a frosty morning, welcoming him, urging him to linger. Her caress, her touch spoke eloquently, telling him of her hunger, of her desire to bring him enjoyment.

How firm yet how pliant her breasts felt cupped in his hands, touched by his mouth. How sweet the taste of her nipple against his stroking tongue.

Such simple things she'd given him as they made love, such breath-catching pleasure they brought ... her soft moans and unconscious sighs, the slow rocking movements of her hips, her cry of fulfillment.

Abruptly Steve was brought back to the present, realizing the intimate touch he'd been remembering was no longer just a memory.

"When was the last time you spent the entire day in bed, Maddox?" Danielle asked.

He groaned and reached for her, as filled with needing and wanting her as he had been the night before. "Ask me that question tomorrow," he said, his mouth closing over hers.

THE SATURDAY they had spent making love became a bittersweet memory for Danielle as summer moved into New York with the tenacity of a tax collector and as Steve became more and more consumed by the problems facing Eagle Enterprises—problems that forced him to leave town for weeks at a time.

The dry heat in Nevada had seemed mild in comparison to the humid, greenhouse feeling of New York City in the summer. It was on a particularly hot day, during a trip back from the airport, where she had gone to see Steve off, that she first noticed she was having trouble catching her breath. The episode passed but came back again the next day, and the next, until her long deep sighs eventually became as natural to Danielle as her normal breathing.

Weeks passed, each indistinguishable from the next, marked only by the check marks she made in her little black book beside the museums or galleries or restaurants she visited.

Elaine returned to New York from Texas for three days at the end of July. She and Danielle went shopping together and finally managed to have lunch at the Plaza Hotel, where they examined the portrait of Eloise that hung on the wall. It was the only time Danielle had company on one of her excursions.

As summer began to nudge fall, Danielle found she was having more and more trouble sleeping. Each week that Steve had to be away, he flew home to spend some time with her; once he was home less than six hours before he had to leave again. She watched him closely for signs of fatigue, but saw only the vibrant good health of a man who appeared to thrive on what would be a killing pace to most.

Steve arrived home early one evening in mid-September to find Danielle sitting in the middle of her bed with catalogs and pamphlets spread out around her. He came across the room to give her a kiss; she pulled him down beside her, their bodies causing a crackling sound as they rolled across the strewn papers.

Propping himself up on an elbow, Steve looked down at her. "What's all this?"

"I've been thinking about signing up for some classes. I never had a chance to go to college after high school, so I figured, why not now?"

Her statement was innocent enough, even reasonable. Then what was it that made Steve feel uneasy? "Isn't it too late to sign up for this semester?"

"So I've discovered." Her laugh sounded brittle. "I just thought there might be a way I could still get in without transcripts and all the rest—some loophole that pertained to us last-minute, out-of-town types."

"Maybe you could take private lessons in something. There are dozens of cooking schools. How about painting, or some kind of craft?"

Danielle winced. "I guess I did make it sound like I was just looking for something to do."

"Did you see the doctor today?" he asked softly.

She nodded. "He actually laughed when I told him we had been married almost four months and I was getting concerned about not being pregnant yet. But he examined me anyway. He said there was no reason I couldn't have a dozen children if I wanted them."

"Do you want me to go in to see him?"

"Why? So he can have another laugh?" Danielle's arm covered her eyes. "He said to wait for a year and then come back if we're still having trouble."

Steve kissed the hollow at the base of her throat. "He isn't the only gynecologist in New York, Danny. Go to another if you would feel better about it."

She rolled to her side, away from him. "I would in a minute," she said softly, "if I felt the answer would be any different."

"Are you worried about waiting another year because of your age? Because if you are, you don't have to be. I've been doing some reading about pregnant women in their thirties and it's—"

"Oh, Steve, it's not that!" *Dammit*, she was crying again. Surreptitiously she wiped away the tears. "Steve...how would you feel about letting Zelda go?" She held her breath as she waited for his reply, trying to will him to say what she so desperately wanted to hear. She felt him move, and guessed that he had turned to lie on his back.

"Why?" he asked.

The way he said the single simple word dampened her hopes. Yet she went on, "We hardly create enough mess around here for maid service once a month, let alone three times a week."

"Are you sure that's the real reason?"

"Yes . . . no." Suddenly needing Steve's warmth, Danielle rolled over and pressed herself into his side. "I feel like I'm an intruder when she's here." She shrugged. "School is obviously out of the question, at least for now. Steve, I simply can't keep finding new things to do so that I'm not here twelve days every month."

"What does Zelda do when she's here that makes you feel so uncomfortable?"

"That's just it. She doesn't do anything. Oh, Steve, I know how foolish this sounds. A bad-tempered bull couldn't intimidate me at the ranch, yet here I am letting a woman who's hired to do the cleaning run me out of my own home."

"Could it be that you're uncomfortable with someone else doing what you've always done for yourself?"

"I suppose that's part of it . . . there's no reason I couldn't take care of this place myself." She had to force the next words; somehow saying them aloud seemed so wrong. "I don't have anything else to do."

The silent seconds became minutes. "I'm sorry it's been so lonely for you this summer—it isn't what I had planned. I thought we would have more time together. I had no way of knowing all hell would break loose like it did. When I came back to New York that week before we were married I even made a list of friends we could invite for dinner parties, so that you'd have a chance to meet people. None of it seemed to work out."

Danielle's arm tightened around his waist. "Steve, I'm not complaining. I know how things got out of hand."

"It will be better this winter. I promise. We'll entertain as frequently as you like."

"I have to find something to do with myself in the meantime. . . ."

"Most of the accounts seem to be settling down. There's not much on the calendar."

"And Zelda?" she asked softly.

"Maybe it would help you understand why it's hard for me to let her go if I told you how she came here in the first place." Steve ran his hand through her hair, absently combing the long strands with his fingers. "About four years ago, we did some consulting work on a small restaurant chain here in the city. Zelda's husband, Harold, was one of the employees we recommended letting go. The loss of his job precipitated a heart attack. Zelda came to my office wanting to know who had given me the right to play God in people's lives. She wanted to know how she was going to feed and clothe her children...." He sighed heavily. "She wanted to know a lot of things."

"So you gave her a job," Danielle said.

"Her husband has never been able to go back to work."

"Surely you don't blame yourself for that?"

"It's so easy to rationalize sacrificing a few people's jobs to save the majority when it's done on a piece of paper. In real life it's a little more difficult. Especially when the economy is in the shape it's in now and you know that the chances of those people finding other jobs is damn near nil."

"I understand...."

"Danny?" He brought his hand to her chin and forced her to look at him. "If you want me to let Zelda go, I will. I only wanted you to understand why it wouldn't be easy for me. I didn't want to make you change your mind."

"I know." And she did. "Let's give it a while longer. Maybe I haven't tried hard enough."

He turned to her; the pamphlets beneath him crackled softly. "Nothing is as important to me as you are."

"I know," she whispered, fighting an overwhelming sadness she didn't fully understand. His lips were suddenly demanding against her own. Or was he merely responding to her own desperate need?

DANIELLE FACED the following weeks with renewed determination. Then in late November Steve was called out of town again; he was to be gone for four days. During his absence she initiated her own self-discipline program. Daily, hourly she reminded herself of the agony he had borne alone in Vietnam, of the long months he had stayed at the ranch when he'd come home. Surely if he could give an attempt at adjustment so much time, she reasoned, so could she. Only this time the end result would be different. She would win.

After she had completed her weekly telephone call to the ranch that Saturday morning, she sat perfectly still for a long time, her hand resting on the receiver. If she were ever going to truly become a New Yorker, she was going to have to start looking like one. Before she could change her mind she again picked up the phone and dialed the number of the exclusive beauty salon Elaine had recommended, making an appointment to have her long hair shaped into something more fashionable.

To keep her mind off the late-afternoon haircut she went shopping, taking advantage for the first time of the assortment of credit cards Steve had insisted she carry, trying to modify her still-powerful resistance to using his money. When the time for her appointment finally arrived, Danielle took a deep breath and stepped from the limousine, telling the driver she would take a taxi back to the apartment so he could go to the airport to pick up Steve.

Two and a half hours later Danielle stepped back onto the sidewalk in a daze. Surreptitiously she turned to catch a glimpse of herself in the glass door, and caught the glance of the woman who was relocking it behind her. In mime the woman patted her own hair, pointed to Danielle and made a circle with her thumb and index finger.

Numbly Danielle nodded, her return smile wooden. Automatically she reached up to brush back stray tendrils caught by the light wind. Her hand went to waves that were no longer there.... A geometric cut, the man with the scissors had called it. Danielle closed her eyes to shut out the image in the glass. Whatever the style was called, it hadn't left her with hair much longer than Steve's. She felt exposed, naked as she turned toward the curb to hail a cab.

Large drops of water splattered on her outstretched hand and Danielle glanced skyward. Somehow it seemed supremely fitting that after holding off all day, rain should start falling at that precise moment. Within seconds it was pouring. She ducked back into the salon doorway for cover, assuming the shower would soon subside and she could go back to hailing a taxi without getting soaked.

After a quarter of an hour had passed and there was no sign of a let-up, she trudged back to the curb. Nothing she was wearing would be ruined by the rain, not even her new haircut. "Wash and wear," the man had said repeatedly as his scissors cut closer and closer to her scalp. "You're just going to *love* it," he had promised, ignoring her initial request—that her hair be left long enough for her to wear pinned on top of her head. And when she'd commented about the length, his cool reply had been, "I understood you wanted it styled, not barbered."

The river of yellow cabs—all occupied—flowed past, as unresponsive to Danielle's gestures as the stylist had been to her request. Ten minutes later she realized it wasn't only the clouds that made the sky so dark, it was the late hour. She gave up and headed for a bus stop.

Standing under a printed bus schedule that had been bolted to a steel pole, she glanced from it to her watch. If both were accurate, she had a ten minute wait. A sudden thought made her shake her head and groan in frustration. She couldn't ride a bus without the correct change, and since coming to New York she'd made it a habit to take the change out of her purse to make it lighter.

She carried the small bag at Steve's insistence—part of the survival rules he had made her learn. A purse must be held tightly under her arm, with the strap over her shoulder. Thieves in New York, he had told her, preyed on the unwary.

And jewelry. She shouldn't flaunt her wealth by wearing anything too flashy on the street. That too was bait.

And eye contact. It had taken her a while to grasp the idea that what was considered friendly in Nevada, was a "come on" in New York.

Finally, but only after several uncomfortable incidents, she had learned to travel the streets like a native—eyes forward, walking what seemed like twice her normal speed, adroitly brushing past the oncoming throng instead of bumping into them.

By now the rain was running in tiny rivulets down her collar, wetting her uncomfortably. Again, Danielle retreated to a doorway while she searched her purse for coins.

As she lowered her head she caught a movement from the corner of her eye—and what followed next seemed to happen in a crazy mixture of slow motion and incredible speed. A man in dark clothing—maybe olive green turned black by the rain, she noted inconsequentially—approached her. One hand was at his side, the other tucked in his unzipped jacket. He stepped in front of her and the hidden hand flashed into view—holding a narrow-bladed knife. As if executing the graceful follow-through of a ballet movement, the knife-wielding hand moved toward her. Even in the dim light the blade shone with a menacing gleam. Danielle felt a light tug across her shoulder. The man turned and fled the way he had come.

It felt like long minutes before she realized what had happened, but in reality it was only seconds. He had taken her purse at the same instant he had cut the strap. Fury replaced her momentary confusion. Before the thief had traveled half a block, Danielle was running after him.

"Stop him!" she shouted. "He stole my purse!" But in the downpour no one seemed to hear or react. Everyone was huddled under umbrellas, hurrying to reach shelter. *Rule number twelve*, she inwardly seethed. *Never count on help from strangers.*

Danielle had run at least a block when suddenly her heel caught in a sidewalk grating. She sprawled forward, catching herself with her hands on the cement.

Automatically, as if she'd just taken a tumble from a horse, she got to her feet again. But the man had disappeared.

It was as if all her frustration, her anger, her hurt and disappointment in the last months had found voice in her rage over losing her purse. She had refused to consider what she would do if she caught up to a man who was not only a head taller, but who probably outweighed her by fifty pounds as well. All she'd wanted was the satisfaction of feeling she had come out the winner at least once since she had been in this city. Danielle looked down at her palms, which were scraped and bleeding. Her knees were raw as well, and her stockings torn. In her sodden state she looked a mess—and felt worse.

The salty tears that mixed with the sooty rain on her cheeks had nothing to do with the loss of her purse. It was as if the last unbroken rung of the ladder that had been holding her out of the well of despair had finally snapped. No longer would she be able to convince herself that all she needed was a little more time and everything would be all right. It wouldn't be, not until she got back to some wide open spaces again. This city chewed people like her up—people who needed to feel the earth. Each day that she'd stayed, another tiny piece of her had died. She wasn't tough enough to live here the way she'd been doing. The city had won.

Danielle looked up to see a woman watching her. The instant their eyes met the woman looked away, and Danielle instinctively knew that if she asked her for money to make a phone call, she would be ignored. Slowly she walked to the corner to get her bearings, mentally figuring which direction she should travel and how long it would take her to walk home.

"My God, Danny," Steve gasped. "What happened to you?" He reached for her, pulling her into the apartment and into his arms. "You're like a piece of ice." He pushed the door closed, bent and lifted her into his arms.

"I got lost...."

"Why didn't you call?"

"A man stole my purse."

He took her into the bedroom and began removing her clothes. "Why didn't you—"

"Steve...please don't." Her throat tightened convulsively.

He stopped to look at her. "I'm sorry," he whispered. Suddenly, as surely as if she had already spoken the words aloud, he knew. He saw it in her eyes, in the defeated set of her shoulders. But to know something is not always acceptance. He held her face between his hands, his thumbs gently caressing her chin. "I was so scared, Danny. I was terrified that something had happened to you."

"Something did happen...."

A sure and dreaded knowledge of what she would say next made him stop her words by pressing his mouth to hers. The kiss they shared, so filled with poignancy, added to his dread. She was so cold. He held her closer, trying to give her heat from his body. "I love you," he told her. Over and over he said the words, seeking the tone, the urgency, the longing that would express the depth of his feelings for her, all the while knowing it wouldn't express the depth of his feeling for her, all the while knowing it wouldn't make any difference. There were no words. He knew no way to reach into the depths of his heart, his very soul, and convey to her what was there.

To say he couldn't go on without her implied he would cease to exist if she left. He would not. But there was something deep inside of him that would die. And this time if they should part, the pain would be that much keener for the promise that would die with it. He would be alone again, only the loneliness this time would not have edges softened by memories that were ten years old.

Danielle leaned her head against his chest. She had begun to shiver, and goose bumps covered her arms and legs. "Steve, we have to talk...."

He had known this was coming and he had tried to deny it, telling himself the unhappiness he saw in her eyes would fade in time. How easily he had convinced himself that it would only take a little more time and she would adjust to the strange new world he had introduced her to. How easily? No, how desperately.

Steve reached for the quilted bedspread, pulling it from the bed and wrapping it around Danielle. Tenderly he kissed her forehead. "First we get you warmed up—then we talk." *Ten points for behaving in such a normal manner while your world falls apart around you, Maddox.* He made her sit on the edge of the bed while he went in to run a warm bath. Like rapidly fired bullets, arguments he would use to keep Danny from leaving raced through his mind as he waited for the tub to fill. He would not—he could not—let her go.

But when he walked back into the bedroom and saw her, twin streams of tears running down her cheeks, he knew he would use none of the arguments. "Danny," he said softly as he came to her and touched her face, "what happened to your hair?" All the sunshine had been taken from her hair, leaving a dark brown cap that clung to her head. Even though he didn't want to hear her answer, he had to ask.

She looked at him. "I thought...." She shrugged; the blanket moved against her bare neck." I thought if I could make myself look like someone who really belonged here, I would feel like I did." She sniffed and wiped away the moisture from her eyes; new tears immediately appeared. "It didn't work.... It was almost as if the city was laughing at me." She tried to laugh too, but it became a sob. "I was robbed, I fell down, no one would let me use their phone or lend me the money to call you.... I got lost."

"You can't blame—"

"I'm not, Steve. This is a wonderful place for millions of people. But you have to be tough to live here—or something. I guess I'm just not tough enough."

"We could move—"

"To Nevada?" She didn't wait for him to reply because she already knew the answer. "It isn't just the city, Steve," she said softly. "If it were, we could work something out." The words were so difficult to say. "I've never been an appendage before. Until we married, I was a whole person. I worked, and the work I did was important and fulfilling. Now I only feel complete when you're with me. When you're gone, I'm lost. I don't know who I am anymore. There's nothing for me to do here, no way for me to form my own identity." Again she wiped away the tears. "Did you know the only room I ever use when you're not here is the bedroom? There isn't another place in this apartment where I feel comfortable, where I feel I belong. I've never even seen a particle of dust here. Do you have any idea what that's like after living my entire life in Nevada? It's like living in a sterile model home."

She looked at him, her eyes the window to her pain, the mirror of his own suffering. "I'm dying here, Steve. A little more each day I feel something inside of me withering. I won't be the person you fell in love with much longer. I don't even *like* the person—the coward—I've become."

Steve took her in his arms. Each intake of air created a stabbing pain in his chest. Somewhere, somehow he would have to forget the selfish side of his love, the side that demanded she stay, and find a way to let her go. "We'll talk about it tomorrow, Danny. Right now I'm worried about getting you warm again and getting you something to eat."

"Steve—tomorrow won't—"

"One day won't make any difference. What we have to say to each other can wait one more day." He carried her to the bathroom, forcefully keeping his mind off her hair. He couldn't remember ever telling her how beautiful he had thought it. How he had dreamed of its golden highlights flashing in the Nevada sun, how he would sometimes awaken early in the morning while she still slept and stare at the shimmering mass draped across the pillow or lying softly over her shoulder. How he'd often reached out to touch its silkiness. He couldn't tell her now. He would never be able to tell her.

And she had had it cut for him.

While Danielle lay back in the double-sized tile tub, Steve went into the kitchen to fix her some soup. Later he fed her the broth while she sat propped up in bed, and before the bowl was empty her eyelids began to droop.

Steve set the soup aside and helped her to lie down. He then lay down beside her, holding her in his arms while she drifted off to sleep. He held her throughout the night, never leaving her alone. It was the first night in weeks that she did not awaken and sit up, trying to catch her breath as she quietly fought an overwhelming sense of suffocation. When morning came he eased himself from the bed, bathed and dressed for work.

He spent the day clinging to the same thread of hope that controls a condemned man, not phoning for fear of jinxing that hope. Unable to stand being away any longer, he left for home early. The ride to the apartment, through heavier than normal traffic, became nerve-wracking; the seemingly endless ride on the elevator even more so. The instant he opened the door, he understood why. Danny was gone. He felt her loss in the apartment like the absence of sunshine on a summer day.

Slowly he closed the door behind him. How could she leave without saying goodbye? His mind screamed the question while knowing the answer. There could be no goodbye for them. The pain would have been too great.

He went to the bedroom, a wounded man seeking confirmation of his pain. Propped against the pillow was an envelope bearing his name. It took him an hour to perform the motions that would finalize what had been between them. Finally he pulled the flap from the envelope and slowly withdrew the paper folded inside.

My Dearest Steve,
Please forgive me this final act of cowardice. I could not wait for you to come home this evening. I might have stayed if I had. I love you. I will always love you.

Danny

The paper fluttered to the floor as he stood and walked to the window. Rain from the lingering storm made the city lights shine and reflect with a holiday sparkle. Central Park stretched below. He thought of the people who would envy him this view of the city. How hollow his successes suddenly seemed.

The city faded behind a window grown foggy with his deep, convulsive sighs. Slowly his hand went to the pane and with an outstretched, trembling finger, he wrote . . . DANNY WAS HERE.

Once again memories were all he had. They closed around him like old familiar friends, promising little, expecting nothing, forever there.

He had spent the day telling himself that he loved her enough to let her go—how wrong he had been.

11

DURING THE TWO-HOUR layover in Chicago, Danielle called the ranch to make arrangements for someone to meet her in Reno. Ben was waiting when the plane arrived. His hug of welcome was warm and loving and unquestioning. Danielle fought the tears that seemed to have become her constant companions.

"I can't say I'm real happy to see you, Missy," he said.

"I'm not all that happy to be here, Ben." She felt a single drop of moisture escape her eye. Quickly she wiped it away.

He reached for her bags. "What did you do to your hair?" As usual, he had come straight to the point. "I nearly didn't recognize you."

Automatically she reached for the shorn locks. "It's a long story. One that will keep for a winter night in front of the fire."

They made their way through the terminal and parking lot. A tiny smile curved Danielle's mouth when she spotted the beryl-green truck with the double H on the side. She insisted on riding home with the windows down to fill her lungs with the familiar smells of the Nevada desert. Leaning her head against the back of the seat, she closed her eyes and thought of Steve and the cruel way she had left him. *Please forgive me, Steve,* she silently cried. *I had to leave you the way I did or I would not have been able to leave at all.*

Her eyelashes were damp against her cheek. Ben's hand covered hers where it lay on the seat. "Want to talk about it?"

Slowly she shook her head. "No," she whispered. "It hurts too much."

Long minutes passed in silence. Finally Danielle opened her eyes. She ran her hand through her wind-whipped hair. "I think it's harder for me to see my hair so dark than it is to see it short. I never realized how sun-bleached it was until it was all gone."

"You just recently had it done?"

"Yesterday." Was it really only a day ago?

He glanced her way "Don't fret about it overly much, Danny. It'll grow back."

She laughed. It was a good thing she hadn't been looking for reassurance that she didn't look as bad as she thought she did. "The haircut taught me a lesson I won't soon forget. The way I figure it, the price wasn't as high as it might seem."

She propped her elbow on the open window. "All the time I was in New York I kept trying to become something I wasn't. In the process I was losing what made me special in the first place. I had trouble remembering who I was. Sometimes I would look at a picture or a statue in a museum and not know whether I liked it because I thought it was pretty or because I thought I was supposed to like it. I tried so hard to be like everyone else, I was like a chameleon."

"And that's why you're here? To figure out who you are again?"

"It's more than that, Ben. While losing my identity, I discovered something about myself I'd never recognized. I need what the ranch gives me as much as I need food to eat and air to breathe. After so many years of working and feeling useful, I can't live a life filled with nothing but leisure. The only days I felt alive were the ones I spent with Steve. I found myself becoming more and more resentful of the demands of his job. I could actually feel myself becoming a nagging, lonely woman. It was only a matter of time until what I was feeling found a voice."

A shudder of revulsion swept through her. "I had to leave before that happened." She bit her lip and looked at the roof of the truck cab, trying to force back a sudden, overwhelming urge to cry. It was as if her capacity for anguish had finally reached its limit. "Oh, Ben," she sobbed. "I love him so much, and it hurts so bad inside...."

DANIELLE SLIPPED BACK into the routine of the ranch as easily as if she had been gone but a weekend. The days became shorter as they neared Christmas, giving her more hours free from mind-numbing chores, more hours to remember what had almost been.

As if by mutual consent, she and Steve did not communicate. Each day that passed without contact made the thought of calling or writing more difficult. As the days and then the weeks went by, a barrier of silence grew between them.

Danielle bought Steve a Christmas present, an original watercolor of a magnificent eagle soaring through a canyon. But she never mailed the package. His birthday came and she made him a shirt. The shirt was never sent. She promised herself spring would be easier.

Steve spent his birthday in Kansas City going over the books of a grain and feed company that was in the process of filing bankruptcy. It was only the second time he had been out of New York in the two months since Danielle had left, a far more normal traveling schedule than the one he had been on the short time they were together.

Unusually weary of searching through ledgers filled with evidence of mismanagement and incompetence, Steve tossed his pencil on the desk and leaned back in the chair. Without the adrenaline-creating spark and challenge he normally felt when faced with a com-

pany's seemingly insurmountable financial problems, his job was little more than another day's work.

He was alone in the accountant's office, having sent
everyone else home for the evening. But then lately,
he acknowledged, he was never able to shake the
feeling of being alone, regardless of where he was or
who he was with. Missing Danny had become such a
familiar ache it seemed as much a part of him as loving her had always been. The fantasy, the part that
seemed not to fit, was the feeling of joy they had
known for such a short time. He sometimes feared the
day would come when he questioned whether or not
the months they'd been together had existed at all.

For days, for weeks after she had gone he had
reached for the phone to call her, to tell her how desperately he missed her, to demand that she return.
And then he would remember her as she had been that
last day and he would return the telephone receiver
to its cradle. She had sacrificed so much for them to
be together; how could he ask that she do it again? To
plead with her to return was to imply that her leaving
had been easy.

Sometimes, when the hurting was at its worst, he
would argue with himself that he only wanted to hear
her voice. But then what would he say? *How's the
weather in Nevada? Did the wholesale beef prices
balance the summer's expenses? Did she too lie awake*

at night, longing to feel him beside her, imagining that they were making love?

How inane would their conversation have to become to keep him from saying words that would only bring pain, words that would make the loneliness more acute?

But, God, how he missed her. Would the hurt never lessen? Again, as he had done over and over recently, he tried to picture what would happen if he were to leave New York and return to Nevada. The scenario never survived past their reconciliation. He couldn't do that any more than she could return to New York. For both of them, where they were had become an integral part of who they were.

But, God, he silently whispered, *how he missed her.*

A self-deprecatory smile twisted his mouth. Steve Zackery Maddox—superstar in the world of business, supposedly able to solve unsolvable problems with little more than a snap of his fingers. A real genius all right, until it came to solving the only problem that mattered—how to bring two people who desperately loved each other back together.

Impatiently he brushed the hair off his forehead, raking long fingers through the thick mass, stopping to rub tension-filled muscles along his neck. He let out a deep sigh and only then realized he had been holding his breath against the swelling pain that gripped him. With sudden clarity he knew the pain he felt would never diminish, the loneliness would never cease. He would never stop loving Danny; he would always ache to have her beside him; for the rest of his life he would remember her laughter, the verbal caress of her sigh. He could not—he would not go on without her. She had tried . . . now it was his turn.

NOT EVEN THE long hours and frantic activity of a ranch shaking itself free from winter lethargy helped lift the heaviness of missing Steve from Danielle's heart. She carried her aching loneliness with her as if it were a natural and lifelong part of her being. She was never without the hurt, never without the poignant memories.

Toward the middle of March, after a particularly exhausting day, Ben walked with Danielle from the barn back to the house. "I'm getting real worried about you, Danny," he said. "If you don't start eating right, you're going to blow away come the next big wind. What's it been, three, four months since you came back? Shouldn't you be perking up a little by now?"

"I always lose weight this time of year," she said, the lie coming too easily. "As soon as things settle down, I'll put the missing pounds right back on."

"Who you trying to kid? It isn't this ranch that's wearing you down."

She would have been able to pull her pretense at normalcy off if he hadn't put his arm around her shoulders. But the warm and loving contact touched a place in Danielle that ached to be touched and she lost the rigid control she had managed to maintain over the long months since her return. She couldn't walk another step. Ben took her in his arms and for once in her life, Danielle didn't care if every ranch hand on the place saw her break down. The pain was too great, the longing to be comforted too powerful. Great heaving sobs wracked her, shaking her thin shoulders.

Several minutes passed before the emotional storm was over. "I'm . . . all right now . . ." she hiccuped against his chest. Ben handed her his handkerchief, instructing her to wipe her eyes and blow her nose. She glanced up, her lashes stuck together in moist triangles, her eyes red and puffy. She tried to smile. "Got more than you bargained for, didn't you?"

"Come on," he said gently. "Let's get a cup of coffee." He kept his arm around her waist until they were in the kitchen, only releasing her to start the coffee.

When they were both sitting at the kitchen table, their elbows propped up before them, their hands wrapped around warm mugs, he urged her to talk to him, to stop holding onto her sorrow like it was a rare treasure.

She stared at the dark liquid in her cup, letting the fragrant steam rise to her swollen eyes. "I anticipated that it would be hard to get through the winter . . . but somehow I didn't think it would be this hard." She glanced from her cup to Ben's concerned eyes. She saw the deep lines etched on his face, the wisdom the years had brought to his eyes. With a start she realized she was probably closer to this quiet unassuming man than she had ever been to her own father. She took a deep shuddering breath. "Whatever happened to 'time heals all wounds'?"

"You should've known better, Danny. The years you spent apart the first time didn't work any miracles. Whatever made you believe it would this time?"

"I had to have something to cling to."

"And now reality has stomped in, is that it?"

She pressed the warm cup to her forehead, trying to ease the throbbing headache her tears had created. "I miss Steve so desperately there are days I think about abandoning everything and going back. But then I remember the reasons I left. There's no solution, Ben. There is no answer."

"Did either of you ever hear of compromising?"

"Steve could no more move back here than I can live there. I know that now. He loves Eagle Enterprises as much as I love this ranch. If he moved back here, he would suffer the same slow death that I went through in New York."

"I didn't say 'give in.' I said, 'compromise.'"

"I don't understand—"

"Seems to me if the two of you didn't have such monumental stubborn streaks you could've come up with some way that you could both give a little and each come up the winner."

"How?" The word was more a plea than a question.

"That I can't tell you," he said, his voice filled with compassion. "It's something the two of you have to work out for yourselves. All I know for sure, Missy, is that you can't go on like you have been. And I can't imagine it's been any easier for Steve than it has been for you."

BEN'S WORDS BECAME her constant mental companions during the next few days. They held the only glimmer of hope she had allowed herself to feel. They were her light in the window, her lifeboat on a storm-tossed sea. Suddenly, early one sun-filled morning while she stared out the window and washed her few breakfast dishes, she realized she had begun to use that precious thread of hope as a promise for tomorrow instead of making something happen today.

As long as there was hope, the day passed easier. To actually do something about that hope was to risk losing it. She closed her eyes and gave a frustrated sigh. Her jaw clamped tightly in self-anger. She had become even more of a coward than she realized. And she had daily died the coward's death her father had warned her about.

Tossing the dishtowel down on the drainboard, Danielle left the kitchen and went into the ranch office. Without pausing to consider the possible consequences of her actions, she dialed the offices of Eagle Enterprises. A woman's voice, a voice with a distinct New York accent that brought back a flood of memories, answered.

"Mr. Maddox's office please," Danielle said. She felt lightheaded; her heart beat heavily in her chest.

"This is Mr. Maddox's office, Rachel Wilcox speaking...." Another accent, this time British.

"Is Mr. Maddox in?" Danielle's own voice sounded shaky. How strange that in all the time she had lived in New York she had never called Steve's office.

"I'm sorry, Mr. Maddox is in a meeting this morning. Would you care to leave a message?"

A message? What kind of message could she possibly leave? That she loved him? That she died a little each day they were apart? Those were words she had to say to him herself. "No, there's no message. Just tell him that Danny called."

"Is there a last name?"

"He'll know who I am."

Slowly she replaced the receiver. The word *disappointment* had taken on a new intensity of meaning.

So close. She had been so close to hearing his voice. And now she would have to wait. *Would he get the message?* Of course he would. *Would he return her call?* She had to believe that he wanted to hear from her as much as she had longed to hear from him. *Then why hadn't he called?* Why hadn't she before now?

They had been through all of this before. There was only one way to survive, they both knew that—it had to be a clean break. What would he think when he learned that she had called? What thoughts would race through his mind?

The phone rang. Danielle jumped, yanking her hand from the receiver as if the sound had carried a charge of electricity. Immediately, she reversed the action and reached for the phone. "Hello?" she said.

"Danny?" It was Steve.

She caught her breath. "Steve?"

"Did you just call me?"

"Yes . . . your secretary said you were in a meeting."

"She interrupted the meeting—"

"That wasn't necessary. She didn't have to disturb you." *Was she really saying these things?*

"It's all right, it wasn't an important meeting. . . ." He paused. When she didn't say anything, he went on, "Did you want something—"

"I think we should talk, Steve. There are things we need to . . . there are problems we should. . . ." Why hadn't she at least taken a few minutes to figure out how to tell him she wanted to see him?

Three thousand miles away Steve felt a sudden, piercing jolt in the pit of his stomach. "What are you trying to say, Danny?" he asked, his fear making his words sound cold.

And then Danielle knew a dread of her own. Was it possible he had learned to live without her—that he didn't have the overwhelming need to be with her that she had to be with him? Could that be the reason he hadn't called—that he simply hadn't wanted to?

"I just thought...." She swallowed, trying to loosen the lump she felt in her throat. "I was wondering...." Dammit, what was wrong with her? "Are you going to be coming out this way some time in the near future? We have several things we should discuss and I thought it might be better if we did that in person rather than over the phone."

Where his hand held the phone, the knuckles grew white. Where his other hand rubbed his forehead, it did so with such force it left a reddened patch of skin. Had he let too much time pass? Would he be able to convince her that it was still possible for them to build a life together, even after she had reached the conclusion it was better to finalize their separation?

After a long pause, he said, "As a matter of fact, I have a meeting in San Francisco next week."

Again she swallowed. "I think we should get together...if you can arrange it in your schedule to meet me."

"Danny...." He said her name with such loving tenderness she had to blink back tears of longing. "How can you say such a thing? Can you really believe I wouldn't find or make time to see you?"

"It's been so long...I didn't know how you would feel about seeing me again. The way I left was so cruel—I wasn't sure if you'd forgiven me."

"That's behind us now." His even tone did little to reassure her. He had always been so good at hiding his feelings, especially the ones that had caused him the greatest pain. He went on to tell her when and where they would meet, adding that if she wanted to spend the entire weekend, he would arrange a room for her at the hotel where he was staying.

Would she want to stay? Could she stand being so near him when the barrier their long silence had created stood between them like a wide, yawning canyon?

The next eight days were the longest she had ever known.

12

DANIELLE PACED the lobby of the Fairmont Hotel. She had purposely arrived early, thinking she could use the extra time to compose her thoughts. Instead, once she had gone to her room and unpacked her small bag, she found herself compulsively watching the numbers turn on the digital clock beside the bed, growing more and more nervous as the time they were to meet drew nearer and nearer. She had finally given up and gone downstairs to wait.

Standing in front of the registration desk, Danielle glanced at her watch and noted she still had ten minutes to go. She considered returning to her room and checking her appearance one last time. She wanted to look her best; she wanted Steve to think her beautiful. She had chosen her clothing carefully, taking a week to make her final decision and winding up with a suit of deep forest green silk that made her skin look bronze instead of just suntanned. She had bought the suit on her last day in New York. It had never been worn.

The blouse was a soft white silk, handmade and imported from Europe. Tiny white on white flowers and cutwork decorated the bodice, collar and cuffs. It was only after she had returned to the ranch, and her days and attitudes had slipped back into their lifelong patterns, that she had registered shock over owning a piece of clothing as expensive as that blouse had been. But it was the most beautiful one she had ever seen, let alone owned, and she had never regretted her impulsive purchase. That very morning as Ben had driven her to the airport he had complimented her on her appearance, especially mentioning the blouse. She had avoided telling him the price.

As she turned to walk back to the elevator, she saw Steve come through the entrance doorway. Her heart leaped to her throat, and a sharp pain shot through her chest. Dressed in jeans, boots, a sweater and a tweed jacket, he was breathtakingly handsome. How could she possibly have forgotten what an incredibly good-looking man he was?

The familiar sweep of hair covered his forehead, and he reached up to brush it back as he strode toward her.

"Hi," he said.

She smiled nervously. How desperately she wished he would touch her, if only in friendship. "Hi," she answered.

"Been waiting long?"

"No," she lied.

"Are you ready?"

"Ready?" she repeated dumbly.

"I have something I want to show you." His manner seemed brusk, almost as if he were in a hurry to get through their meeting and on to something else.

Danielle shrugged. "I didn't have any other plans, if that's what you mean."

"Then let's go."

He walked beside her, their hands almost but not quite touching. Danielle fought the crushing feeling of disappointment. What had she expected? Had she really thought she could walk out of Steve's life and then back in again four months later and find him the same warmly affectionate man she had left?

She allowed her fingers to brush against his. He reacted to the seemingly accidental contact as if he had been burned, shoving his hand in his pocket as though protecting himself from the possibility of further pain.

The taxi ride was distressingly quiet. After her inquiry about Elaine, Steve's cryptic, "She's fine," and a comment about San Francsco's cool weather that he replied was normal for that time of year, Danielle stopped trying to make conversation.

They stopped in front of a towering office building. Carefully tended and trimmed shrubs in concrete and stone containers rimmed the building, softening its cool gray facade, making it seem less intimidating. Steve paid the driver, then reached for Danielle's hand to help her from the cab.

His own hand was freezing. But Steve's hands were rarely ever cold—only when he was frightened or terribly upset about something. They had always been the barometer to his emotions. Yet he looked so calm, so controlled.

He led her up a short flight of stairs and over to a bank of elevators. Once inside, they were alone for the first time. He pressed the button for the twenty-eighth floor, releasing her hand and folding his arms across his chest, and she heard him quietly sigh. It sounded like . . . *like the sighs she had breathed in New York.* Her head jerked up and she stared at him. To someone who didn't know him well, nothing would seem out of the ordinary. To Danielle, he suddenly looked more apprehensive than she had ever seen him.

Again he quietly tried to catch his breath. She started to put her hand on his arm, but then the elevator bell sounded and the door opened. He lightly touched the small of her back. "This way," he said, pointing down a short hallway. They came to the end and turned.

Danielle stopped and stared when she saw the door at the end of the second hallway. Confusion, hope, fear swept through her senses like undisciplined storms. Written on the door in sedate gold leaf was the name Eagle Enterprises. She turned to Steve, her eyes full of question. "I don't understand what this means," she said.

"Before you had a chance to ask me about a divorce, I wanted you to see this. I wanted you to know there was a way, a reason for us to try again."

"A divorce?" she breathed. "I didn't come here to...." How could he have believed something like that? "I came here desperately hoping we could find some way to be together. I can't go on without you anymore. My life has been so empty—"

"My God, Danny, I've been going through hell since you called. I thought you had decided to make the break final, that that was why you wanted to meet, what you wanted to discuss."

"I was trying to tell you how much I loved you, how I needed to be with you! But it all came out so wrong. And then, when you sounded so cool, I was afraid I had somehow lost you."

"And yet you came—"

"I had to—"

His trembling hand gently touched her face, the fingers stroking the softness of her cheek, the lines of her chin, the swell of her lips. "I must have dialed your number a hundred times since you left," he said softly, "selfishly ready to beg you to come back to me. For such a long time I was blinded by everything that had happened. I couldn't see a solution. I only knew how much it hurt to be without you. Yet there seemed no way to resolve what stood between us. Every time someone came into my office asking for help it became a bitter paradox that I could solve their problems, yet not solve my own." He looked deeply into her eyes, sending her a message that went beyond his words, telling her of the pain he had suffered, the loss he had felt.

"I don't know if what I've done is enough," he said. "Or even if it was the right thing to do. I only know it was the one way I could find to give you back some of what you had given me."

"Just what is it that you've done?" she asked.

Nervously he reached up to brush back his hair. "Come on...I'll show you." They continued their short journey to the end of the hall, where Steve opened the door, then stepped aside to let Danielle enter first. She walked into a large reception area paneled in white oak and carpeted in deep rust, but otherwise bare. Another door led to a hallway and the entrances to several offices. Steve guided her into one of the offices. She walked over to the window.

Before her was a panorama of San Francisco Bay— to the right the Oakland Bay Bridge, to the left the Golden Gate Bridge, half shrouded in fog. In the center lay Alcatraz Island, its isolated pristine beauty belying its troubled past. Danielle silently watched as container ships passed each other in the harbor, giant lengths of steel slicing the water amongst a scattered assortment of sailboats, their sails seeming like bits of wind-blown paper on the water.

"Well?" Steve asked expectantly.

She wasn't sure what he wanted her to say. "It's beautiful," she answered, but realized the instant she again looked at him that it wasn't what he had wanted to hear. "Steve? Why did you bring me here?"

He came up beside her. "To show you what I've done."

Danielle felt as though they were two records spinning at different speeds. "Steve, you're going to have to *tell* me what it is you've done or I'm going to assume you're taking credit for the San Francisco skyline. Perhaps what I'm really saying is that I've decided to stop jumping to conclusions."

Steve turned so that his back was against the window. Sitting on the wide ledge, his long legs stretched out in front of him, he looked up at her. "Of all the places I've been in my wanderings, San Francisco had always held a special fascination for me." The earlier twitch grew into a slow smile that curved his mouth. "When it finally occurred to me how close this city was to Weberstown, Nevada, it took on an incredible appeal. I wanted to call you as soon as the idea to move Eagle Enterprises out here occurred to me. Hell, I wanted to call you just to hear your voice. But I couldn't. I even had Jerry land in Carson City once, but came to my senses before I left the plane. I couldn't think of any way to tell you about all of this—" he waved his hand, indicating the empty office "—without making it sound like I was bargaining for your love."

Danielle stared out the window, no longer able to watch the naked pain that had come over Steve's face as he talked to her.

"I told myself that I had to do this for you, that it had to be an accomplished fact before I came to you hat in hand." Danielle heard him give a small deprecatory snort. "Yet you saw how quickly I returned your call. It was as if all my fine resolve had been nothing more than a pile of feathers waiting for a wind."

"How much longer would you have to wait before you called me?" Danielle asked.

"Two months—" when he heard her sharp intake of breath, he quickly went on "—if I could have lasted that long. I wanted to bring you here with everything finished."

"It seems to me that all you need is some furniture...."

"You should have seen everything last week. The lease on this place wasn't due to come through for another month. If you go out and touch the gold leaf on the door, you'll discover the varnish is still tacky." He reached for her hand, mutely asking her to look at him. "Now that you know what I had in mind, I guess it comes down to whether or not you think you can put up with a weekend husband," he softly said.

"You've moved the entire operation out here?" She was stunned by the enormity of his gift of love.

"What's left of it. When I told them I planned to cut back drastically on the number of new clients the firm would be taking on, half of our employees opted to stay in New York. Eagle Enterprises is as small or as large as I want it to be, depending on the number of clients we accept. It took me a while to realize I no longer needed the frantic activity to keep me from missing you, but old patterns are sometimes hard to break." His hand closed tighter around hers. "It will be a few months before the actual work load lessens appreciably, but I promise you I'll never again allow myself to get caught up in the merry-go-round I was on last summer."

"Steve—"

"This is nothing like the way I had it planned, Danny," he said. "I had something entirely different in mind when I pictured this moment. I imagined myself driving up to the ranch, sweeping you off your feet with the news of what I had done and dramatically carrying you off into the sunset. I was even ready with answers for every possible protest you might make that my crazy scheme for a commuter marriage wouldn't work." His gaze caressed her. "There was absolutely no way that I was going to take 'no' for an answer. Not then . . . not now."

She sat down beside him on the ledge, smiling to herself at the challenge she heard in his voice. "I discovered something about myself this last month," she quietly admitted. "It seems that when I wasn't looking, some of the big city life must have rubbed off on me. I actually discovered I missed going to plays and seeing the art shows—" She gave him a sheepish grin. "I even missed the shopping." As naturally as if they had never suffered their long and painful separation, Danielle put her arm through his and rested her head against his shoulder. "Have you found an apartment yet?"

"It was next on my list of things to do."

"Do you suppose you could look for one large enough to include an occasional 'middle of the week' wife?" She pulled back to look at him, trying to absorb the reality of being with him again. When she took his hand in hers, it was again warm. "It looks like we won't be needing an extra room at the hotel after all," she said softly. "No sense in paying for something we won't be using."

He grinned. "What extra room?"

"Seems to me that you were pretty sure of yourself, Maddox."

But his answer carried none of her teasing tone. "When I stopped trying to convince myself that I could find a way to exist without you, I knew there was only one possible outcome for today. I even have an incredible assortment of impassioned speeches I'll tell you about sometime."

"Speeches?"

"To convince you that divorcing me was—"

She stopped him by pressing her fingers against his lips. "It's behind us now."

He kissed each of her fingertips. "Are you serious about living here?"

"A very wise man I know suggested we look for a compromise to our problems. A very wise man who sends his love, by the way. Never once did I imagine we would find our compromise this easily."

Steve gently pressed his lips against hers. "Ben is going to make one hell of a grandfather," he murmured.

"Not if we don't start working on making him one."

"You're not suggesting—"

She smiled. She hadn't been "suggesting," but the idea sounded too good to pass up. "Who would ever know?"

"Dammit, Danny," he said, his voice a husky whisper, his eyes filled with a warm smile, "you know what it does to me when you say things like that."

"Just think what a golden opportunity this is. Months from now, when you're here in the office facing a disgruntled client, you'll be able to think about today and—"

"And sit there with this stupid grin on my face."

"And remember—"

"A woman with sunshine in her short curly hair."

"Who loved you on a bright San Francisco morning—'

"And who was loved in return...."

He kissed her then, and Danielle knew that Steve had never seriously considered refusing her. The caviar she had ordered sent to her room at the hotel would have to wait until later. Much later.